STREAMS TO THE RIVER, RIVER TO THE SEA

"A suspenseful, well-paced retelling of this remarkable, true-life adventure."
Library Journal

"An honest, unsparing account . . . intriguing."
Publishers Weekly

STREAMS TO THE RIVER, RIVER TO THE SEA

A Novel of Sacagawea

Scott O'Dell

FAWCETT JUNIPER • NEW YORK

RLI: $\dfrac{\text{VL: 5 \& up}}{\text{IL: 6 \& up}}$

*To the memory of Bernard DeVoto,
helpful friend, teacher, author, historian,
whose ashes are scattered in a red cedar grove
on the Lewis and Clark Trail, near a fork of
the Clearwater River, in the mountain
wilderness he loved.*

Author's Notes

To understand the value of the journey Lewis and Clark made from St. Louis to the Pacific Ocean by way of the Missouri and Columbia rivers, it's necessary to know the reasons the journey was made, reasons that Sacagawea, who tells this story, did not know.

In 1801, Thomas Jefferson, president of the United States, had at least a dozen big problems. But there was only one problem that really worried him. Our country was surrounded by enemies and false friends.

France owned Louisiana. Spain owned Florida and great chunks of our Southwest and wanted to own more. England owned Canada and often cast a covetous eye on Louisiana, which she could easily capture and thus would be able to control and tax the ships that plied the Mississippi.

Jefferson wondered how he could possibly find a way out of this frightening web. His country was still weak after a bloody war with the British. He didn't want to launch another. He thought hard for months and kept his thoughts to himself.

At last, he came up with a wonderful idea. He would ask Congress to buy Louisiana from France. Meanwhile, quietly, carefully, so as not to arouse suspicion, he would gather a band of young adventurers to explore the northeast, a wilderness that no white man had ever seen.

France was poor. Napoleon had gobbled up Europe but had beggared the nation. She was glad to sell Louisiana for the paltry sum of fifteen million dollars—paltry because Louisiana was bigger than the whole United States. Imagine a country that vast!

Jefferson had his band of adventurers, all from the U.S. Army. To lead them, he chose two men. One was Meriwether Lewis, twenty-nine, a tireless youth given to serious thoughts about animals and birds, the look of the land, storm clouds, winding rivers. The other young man, William Clark, thirty-three, was full of laughter. He took every day pretty much as it came and thought himself very lucky to be alive.

Sacagawea (*sak-a-ja-way'-ah*) was a Shoshone, a member of the nomadic tribe of Indians who lived high in the Rocky Mountains. She went with Lewis and Clark, on foot, on horseback, by canoe, four thousand miles on a journey that ranks in courage and danger with any journey of recorded history.

There are many tales about what happened to the Shoshone girl, whom Captain Clark loved and called "Janey." After the long journey she seems to have traveled around a lot in the western mountains. She had two sons, lived for some eighty years, and is buried in the Wind River Valley of Wyoming.

Writing Sacagawea's story, I have used *The Journals of Lewis and Clark*, edited by Bernard DeVoto, Nicholas Biddle's edition of the same journals, and *Lewis and Clark, Partners in Discovery* by John Bakeless.

15 millim. $
for Louisiana Purchase

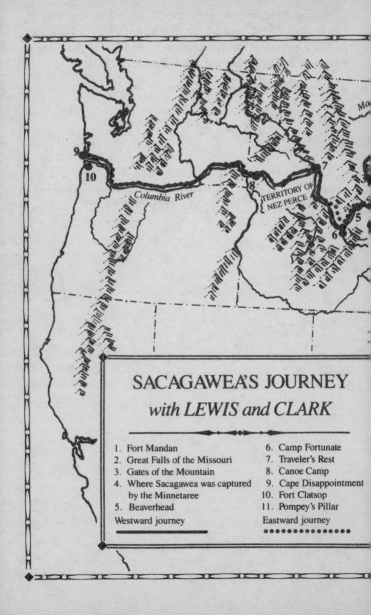

Ma...

Columbia River

TERRITORY OF
NEZ PERCE

9

10

8

7

6

5

SACAGAWEA'S JOURNEY
with LEWIS and CLARK

1. Fort Mandan
2. Great Falls of the Missouri
3. Gates of the Mountain
4. Where Sacagawea was captured
   by the Minnetaree
5. Beaverhead

Westward journey

6. Camp Fortunate
7. Traveler's Rest
8. Canoe Camp
9. Cape Disappointment
10. Fort Clatsop
11. Pompey's Pillar

Eastward journey

Missouri River

Knife River

1

Yellowstone River

11

TERRITORY OF MANDANS

ROCKY MOUNTAINS

Chapter One

Sacagewea and her cousin Running Deer

We were gathering blackcaps on the stream above the place where the three big rivers meet. Summer was almost gone but there were still a few sweet berries hidden deep in the bushes, where bears and deer could not find them.

It was close to dusk. We had come to the stream at early dawn and both of us were weary, almost too weary to talk.

My cousin, Running Deer, said, "Have you heard the squirrels chattering over there on the far bank in that big tree? Not the cottonwood tree, the other tree?"

"Yes, ever since the sun left us," I said.

"Do you hear them now?"

I dropped a handful of blackcaps in the basket and listened. "Not a sound," I said.

"They must hear something."

My cousin was nervous. She was always nervous. When a storm was coming, also when it came, also at nightfall if she was not safe by the fire, she was nervous.

"Squirrels hear a lot of things," I said to calm her. "They have better ears than we do. And they hear more things than we do. Things not worth hearing."

"Don't you think it's time to go?" she asked me.

"A few more handfuls will fill the basket," I said. "Nothing looks more shiftless than a basket that's only half full."

I got down on my knees. I picked faster now. My cousin did not help me. The squirrels had started to chatter again and she was listening.

Suddenly the squirrels were silent.

It was very quiet in the meadow now. I heard nothing save the fuzzy drone of mosquitoes and down the stream the bark of a dog. From the opposite direction and near at hand I heard a different sound—the high, drawn-out cry of a wolf.

Running Deer said, "Wolves. Many of them."

"Only one," I said. "But one can sound like many."

The path back to our camp was through a patch of chokecherries, a fine place for a hungry bear. Bears have a strong smell. But we smelled only roasting meat on the night wind.

We were on an island in the stream. The country around was flat and the stream divided into two forks. The island lay in the middle, covered with cottonwood and quaking aspen. It was easy to go through the trees without being seen. That is why the horsemen did not see us.

They had come from the north, down the right fork of the stream, and now were near the island's edge. They rode silently, two men on spotted horses.

"Who are they?" my cousin whispered.

I knew who they were. "Minnetarees," I said.

The Minnetarees traveled far on their spotted horses. They went out on long hunts, to plunder their neighbors, to kill men, and to capture women and children. They were our hated enemies.

A pair of magpies skittered across the stream and set up a clatter. The men stopped to look at the sky, at the smoke rising above the trees. One of the men was very tall and his hair was cut short to his head—a sign that he was in mourning for someone dead.

I dropped the basket of blackcaps. "Follow me," I said. "We'll go to the other fork and back to camp."

Running Deer started to say something. I held my hand over her mouth.

I had seen that there were more than two horsemen. Minnetarees never raided in twos—always in bands, stealthily, and at suppertime. They had raided us before, once when I was three and another time when I was seven. On these raids they had killed many of our men and carried off eight of our young women and twice that many of our children.

"Hurry," I said. "Come quietly and say nothing."

We waded out to the middle of the stream. Our camp was at the far end of the island. High in the trees I could see the glow of our fires. All the dogs in the camp were barking, which meant that my people were warned.

"Run," I said to my cousin. "Run in the shallows under the trees where the footing is good."

I heard a sharp sound like a tree breaking in the wind, then another sound and another—three altogether. It was the sound firesticks make, the weapons that spit smoke and fire, things the Minnetarees had bought from the white traders.

I overtook Running Deer. "Stay where you are," I told her. "Stay and be silent."

I ran fast in the shallow water. But at a bend in the stream the water grew deep and tugged hard at my legs. I could hardly move.

There were more crackling sounds from the firesticks. Then it was very quiet. But the quiet did not last. The summer grass blazed up and the trees began to burn. A woman screamed.

The burning trees cast a light far up the stream. Night had come on fast, but I could see that our men had left the island and were fleeing north. Close behind them rode a band of Minnetarees on their spotted horses.

I waded out to a sandbar and lay flat in the cold sand.

3

Though there was still a smoldering light in the sky, it was dark where I lay. Some Minnetarees moved out of the camp, driving a herd of neighing horses before them. They shouted Minnetaree words—"Aaagh! Ai, ai, ai!"— boasting of their victory.

Cautiously I got to my feet and started toward the island. I came close to our camp. Grass was on fire. Trees were on fire. Our dead lay everywhere. I saw my mother, dead, and when I screamed, a Minnetaree, the tall one, came out of the cottonwoods. He was dragging Running Deer behind his horse. He threw a noose around my neck and choked me until the night grew black.

passed out

Chapter Two

We rode all night toward the star that shines in the north, the one that never moves. Spread flat on my stomach, I was fastened to the back of a horse. My hands were tied together around the horse's neck by a stout leather rope.

I rode at the very end of the train, the end of the long line of horses and captured women. My captor, the tall one, rode in front of me. He never spoke. Several times when he seemed asleep I thought of leading my horse out of the line, hiding in the woods, and somehow untying the rope that bound me. But what if I failed? What if I was forced to wander for days until I died of thirst, until I was a skeleton tied to a skeleton horse? And what of Running Deer? What would happen to her if I escaped or died?

It was bad to think of escaping and I put it out of my thoughts. Surely my father and my two brothers would be home from the buffalo hunt in a few days. They'd find our camp burned down, the dead people lying in the burned grass, and set off to rescue us.

Near dawn the train halted beside the stream we had been following all night. My captor unbound the ropes and told me to drink because I would not see water again that day.

We were still in the low mountains and it was very cold. The stream ran under a crust of ice. I had to break a hole in it before I could drink and wash my face.

Simile Dawn came as I left the stream. By its light I had my first real look at the Minnetaree. Older than my father, he was a tall, thin man with a small head, round like a melon, which sat squat between his shoulders.

He picked up the rope to tie me and said, touching his chest, "Tall Rock," which I took to be his name. He then spoke a few words, and when he saw that I did not understand them, he made a sign with both his hands, drawing a shape. He rolled his eyes.

He started to pick me up to put me on the horse. As he bent forward I saw hanging from his belt, down the back of his leg, a woman's scalp. The hair was long and black and braided. Through the braids were woven tiny pieces of white fur, ermine fur. It was my mother's hair that hung from his belt.

A scream caught in my throat. Wild words formed on my lips. I said nothing. Quietly I walked to the place where I had made a hole in the ice and washed my hands again and picked up a rock.

The Minnetaree was standing by the horse, mumbling at the delay. When he gathered me up, I brought the rock down on his head. It was a solid blow and he reeled and fell to his knees. I ran for another rock, a bigger one, but as I reached the stream he shoved me from behind so hard that I went crashing through the ice.

After a few moments, while I froze, he dragged me out by my hair, through the sand, through the grass. He tossed me on the horse and bound me again, tighter this time. Then he gave me a good hard slap on both of my cheeks.

We traveled all that day in heavy rain, not stopping until dusk. While I was being untied, Running Deer came to watch, followed by an ugly young Minnetaree with roached

6

hair who stood off at a distance. She was surprised to see me tied up.

"I have a good horse to ride," she told me. "One of our horses. Do you think we can steal away tonight when they're not looking?"

"We don't know the trail," I said. "And the rain has washed out all the footprints the horses have left. We'd be lost before morning."

"That is why, when no one was looking, I broke off twigs all day and dropped them along the trail."

"We can't find twigs in the dark."

"But tomorrow in the daylight they can be found."

"Tomorrow we will see."

I asked her how many of our people were in the train.

"Five or six, I think. Women and boys."

Tall Rock came and stood in front of us and made motions pointing to the way we had come, then drew a finger swiftly across his throat. Running Deer and I did not talk any more.

The next day, while thunder rolled and lightning streaked the sky, one of our women, Little Fox's Daughter, walked away from the train. She had not gone far when the Minnetarees overtook her. I heard a scream and that was all.

My cousin and I never talked again about trying to escape, though she kept breaking off twigs as we rode, dropping them on the trail for our men to see. I kept count of the direction, which was no longer toward the star that does not move but toward the rising sun.

A new moon came and slowly went. We reached running water, the river Missouri, but my father and my two brothers never came to rescue us.

On the morning of the day we first saw the river, the Minnetarees smeared fresh paint on their faces and stripes up and down their chests. And when we reached the river they let out the cries of crazed devils. "Aiyee, aiyee, aiyee!" they shouted, spurring their weary horses.

7

As we rode into their village an old man tottered out to greet us. He had thin, white hair and moved with the help of a stick carved in the crooked shape of an antelope horn. This was the sachem of the Minnetarees, the Father of the People of the Willows, the great chieftain Black Moccasin.

He had a nod for all of his new captives. He went from one to the other of us, squinting his flinty eyes, examining us from head to toe, as if we were mares he was about to buy or had bought and was not quite sure of the bargain.

His gaze lingered on me. I held my breath, knowing that my fate among the People of the Willows was being decided. His gaze shifted away to Running Deer, then came back to me. He had not decided what to do, but Tall Rock, who had waited impatiently, reached out to drag me off. Quick as a snake strikes, the chieftain tripped him with his carved stick and sent Tall Rock sprawling in the dust.

Simile

8

Chapter Three

Minnetarees & Shoshone

The villages that Black Moccasin ruled stretched along the eastern bank of the river for a long way, the distance that twenty well-shot arrows can fly. They were the most wonderful villages I had ever seen or ever heard about.

We, the Agaidüka Shoshone, lived in deerskin huts and moved about in the seasons, from the lowlands to the high mountains. The Minnetarees seldom moved from their villages.

They dwelt in great houses—ten big families could live in just one of them—made of timber and mud. The houses were tight against the deepest snow and the wildest winds. Covered holes in the roof let smoke from the fires drift out. There was also a door, not a flap, a big one that opened and closed. On the outside, each of the houses had a trench dug deep around it to keep out the water when it rained.

Chief Black Moccasin's home was the biggest of all the lodges in the village of Metaharta, though he had only four wives. Three of the wives were kind to me from the very first moment I came into the house. But as soon as Black Moccasin's back was turned, the other wife, Sky Lark, a young Sioux woman, said in sign language, pointing at the earth, "We are enemies and I will see you dead down there."

Chief Black Moccasin knew what she said and gave her a beating with his carved stick. After that she smiled at me if she had a chance and I smiled back, but still I didn't trust her. In truth, I did not trust any of the Minnetarees except Black Moccasin.

That first night I slept little. I had a sleeping place of my own, a corner curtained off with bearskins from the rest of the lodge, but I kept thinking of the burned village I had left and of all my friends, those dead and those living. Especially I thought of Running Deer and the stricken look she had given me when Black Moccasin had shown no interest in her and she was led away by the ugly warrior whose hair was cut short on the sides and stuck up in the middle, the one who had captured her. I lay in the dark and watched the sky beyond the smoke hole, where the stars flowed by in a misty tide. I made peace with the thought that I was now a slave in the country of the Minnetarees and might remain so for the rest of my life.

Fortunately, at dawn I was put to work and had no time to think. The Sioux woman took me out to the drying ground, a level place by the river, and gave me a small deerhide that had been soaking for days.

In sign language she asked me if I had ever worked with deerhides before.

I nodded, making the sweeping sign that means "many."

She said "good" with her hands, twisted her mouth into a doubtful smile, and left me.

I had made leather from the day I was seven years old and every spring and summer and fall since that time. It was hard work but I had always liked it, and I liked it now. As I put the skin down, flesh side up, with pegs two spans of a hand apart, scraped it clear of fat and tissue, and left it to dry, I thought of nothing, save what I had set out to do.

I pegged and cleaned so well that the following day the

Sioux woman brought two skins for me to work with. The next day she brought three. Though I could have done more, I did only two of them. I decided that she wished to make an old woman of me.

I worked at this task day after day until the first birds began to fly south. About this time I made a discovery. I had learned many of the Minnetaree words—it's not a difficult language. By chance one morning while they were cooking breakfast, I overheard the oldest wife and the next to the oldest talking to each other.

Blue Sky, the oldest wife, said, "She has done well for a Shoshone."

"I am filled with surprise," the next to the oldest said. "First, when she came, I had doubts. The big eyes, like a young deer, gave me doubts."

"The Shoshone girls all have big eyes."

"And they know that they do."

"Ai. They know it."

"Their eyes look down and up and sideways, never at you straight."

"The Shoshone girls are shy."

"You think so? Not me!"

I had just awakened and the buffalo robe was pulled up around my face. I pushed it down and listened hard. The women were only a few strides away, standing around the big cooking kettle. A curtain hung between us.

"Red Hawk, my fine son, will be home tomorrow," Blue Sky said. "I heard this from Black Moccasin."

"Then it is true, for Black Moccasin always knows about his son. A spirit tells him all that Red Hawk does."

"And thinks."

"Ai."

"Do you believe that he will like the Shoshone girl? Tell me, what does she call herself?"

"Sacagawea."

11

"What does 'Sacagawea' mean? It makes an odd sound in the mouth."

"Who knows?"

I pushed the buffalo robe away, crawled to the curtain, and set my good ear tight against it. My other ear had been hurt when Tall Rock shoved me into the stream.

"Do you think Red Hawk can like a girl with that sort of name?"

"He has liked many who have worse names than that one. Remember the beautiful Nez Percé girl who called herself One Who Sleeps in the Clouds."

There was a long silence while Blue Sky put wood on the fire and complained that the wood was wet and asked who had gathered it.

"Sacagawea," Second Wife said.

"She should not be gathering wood at this time, with Red Hawk returning so soon. She has done well with the hides. She has proven that she will make a useful wife. Now we must think of helping how she looks."

"Yes, she must look better. Someone chosen to be the wife of a man who will be a chieftain someday, not something wild that's been living in the mountains forever."

There was another silence, the sound of the kettle being stirred, footsteps. I crawled under the buffalo robe and pulled it over my head. My heart sounded like a woodpecker beating on the roof. Me, the mountain girl, the bride of Black Moccasin's son? Sacagawea, Bird Girl, named for the birds I loved and fed when the snows lay deep and the north wind blew. My head spun with dreams.

Blue Sky shouted, "Sacagawea, come!" as if she meant it.

I hurried into my clothes. She was stirring the kettle. She gave me the spoon, an iron spoon. I had never seen such a spoon before I came to live with the Minnetarees. They bought them, and sharp knives too, from the white traders. In the mountains we used spoons made of buffalo bones.

12

My head still spun. But I saw clearly in a wonderful vision a big lodge, my own lodge, with twenty or twenty-one places to sleep, at least ten of them for children, set around the walls, each with its own curtains and wooden pegs to hang clothes on. And by the fire a row of kettles and from three poles nearby I saw iron spoons and dozens of knives hanging.

"Today," Blue Sky said, "we make clothes for you. The thing you wear hurts the eyes. And we will try to do something with your face."

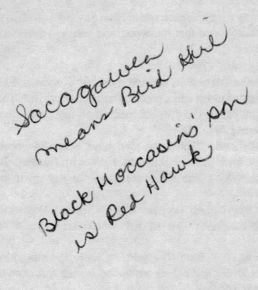

Sacagawea means Bird Girl

Black Moccasin's son is Red Hawk

Chapter Four

The two wives started on me that morning as soon as I had eaten a bowl of mush and a piece of smoked deermeat. They stood me up beside the fire, stripped off all my clothes, and tossed them away.

Blue Sky said, "Shoshone men have beautiful horses, which they wash and comb and trick out with feathers. But their women look like the scarecrows we put up in our cornfields."

"They starve their women also," Second Wife said. "Look at this one. Two of her would scarce cast one shadow."

"None at all," Blue Sky said. "Likely the sun shines clean through her and comes out the other side and casts not the thinnest shadow."

Both of the wives were fat—their legs were bigger than my whole body. The Minnetarees had much food. They planted big fields of corn and squash and beans and had a big storehouse filled with smoked deer and buffalo meat and dried ears of corn, which I had never seen before. The corn tasted good if it was mixed with water and cooked a long time.

The wives called in four women from a different lodge, who were famed in the village as cutters and stitchers. Working as fast as they could, they cut a tunic for me from a beautiful white antelope skin and made a pair of trousers to match it.

They had me stand on a piece of soft deerhide and cut patterns around my feet with a sharp steel knife. In no time at all I had a new pair of moccasins with yellow beads stitched on them and little drags to flop around and make a whispering sound.

The next morning the two wives rubbed me all over with bear grease, even the bottoms of my feet. They washed the grease off and covered me with a scented oil that soon disappeared in my skin, leaving the scent of a prairie rose.

They painted a row of purple dots on my cheekbones and daubed vermilion inside both of my ears. Then they took me outside in the bright sun and gazed at me.

Blue Sky said, "Who would ever believe that what we see there is a Shoshone?"

"No one," Second Wife said. "This must be a spirit child who appears before us."

Blue Sky shook her head. "No, it is not a spirit child we see. This is a dream child, a child we have dreamed, out of, out of . . ."

Second Wife found the word. "Out of little."

They talked together as if I understood nothing of what they said, as if I was not there. So I broke in upon them, politely, though I was angry. "I am what I was before you dressed me up like a doll. I was an Agaidüka Shoshone and I am an Agaidüka Shoshone now. At this moment and forever."

Blue Sky said, "Red Hawk should be pleased with what he finds here."

"Red Hawk can be hard to please sometimes. It is more than twenty summers and winters since he was born and he still is without a single wife."

15

"It's a scandal."

"We've never had a hand in things before. Seven of them he has passed by, one a Sioux princess. But now we shall snare him with our little Shoshone."

"Yes, Black Moccasin took to her when she had a lump on her face and smelled to the clouds. He'll see that his son does likewise."

"Yes, but what reward do we receive for all of our troubles?"

"I will give this some thought."

"Think now. We have little time to waste. Red Hawk appears today. Rewards unasked for fade like morning mist."

I broke in upon them again, raising my voice. "Who is this man who has had twenty summers and twenty winters and not one wife? How does he look, this one who refuses a Sioux princess? To me he sounds spoiled."

All of this I spoke in Shoshone except the part "To me he sounds spoiled," which I said in good Minnetaree with a gesture that means "ugly."

Blue Sky gave me a sharp look. "It is not for you to have thoughts about Red Hawk. You are fortunate if he looks at you twice, even though we have fixed you up. You are fortunate to be taken into Black Moccasin's lodge. That you are not a slave. And two times fortunate that you are not dead."

I swallowed my anger, but it was there simmering in my stomach. It simmered all day while I sat in the lodge waiting for Red Hawk to appear. The two wives would not let me move, fearing that I would spot my beautiful tunic made of the whitest antelope skin and my moccasins that had beads on them and drags that whispered, fearing that I would sweat and the paint on my face would run. They would not let me eat lest I spill something on myself.

The lodge was filled with children who gathered around and stared at me. I sat prettily on two buffalo robes, looking

16

exactly like a princess. I had begun to feel like a princess. But at the end of the day, just as I looked up and saw a star peering through the smoke hole, I heard the thud of hoofs, many of them.

Blue Sky put me on my feet, straightened my tunic, and dabbed some more paint on my face and in my ears. Second Wife brought a pair of moccasins, feathers, and shells and handed me a needle.

"Sew," she said. "It is necessary that Red Hawk sees that you're useful as well as a decoration."

Red Hawk burst through the door, Black Moccasin's arm around him, and gave out a mighty screech: "Ayee, ayee, aaagh!" The children and the wives ran to greet him. Outside, people clamored at the door. Sitting by the fire, I sewed and stitched on the moccasin.

He was tall and thin and very light-colored, like his father, like all the Minnetaree warriors. His hair was black as a blackbird's wing. It hung to his shoulders and swept out like wings as he swaggered to the fire.

There was a hush until he spoke. Then, while he told about how he had brought home enough buffalo meat for two long winters and how he and his men had captured ten Pawnee women and children, the wives kept up a chorus of how brave he was. They clapped their hands and sang something that sounded foolish.

He never looked at me once. But when he had finished his speech and marched outside to repeat it to the crowd, he darted a glance in my direction. One glance and that was all.

It was toward nightfall and a pine tree was burning. Pine, which has a lot of resin, makes bitter smoke. Some of the smoke went out through the roof hole. But most of it stayed in the long house. Running Deer stood close to me but I could barely see her face.

Black Moccasin was by the fire, his favorite place. His wives were busy cooking supper and the children were

17

playing outside. Running Deer spoke softly though no one was listening.

"I have found a way," she said.

"A way to what?" I asked.

"To flee, to go home."

I had seen her in the village, but this was the first time we had talked together. I was surprised that she had come to see me.

"Home?" I asked. "Many of our people are dead. Can you find those who live?"

"I will go and look."

"But why? You have not been harmed by Black Moccasin and his people. You have plenty of food to eat. Winter is near. You will die on the trail."

"You like it here," she said. "You are comfortable here. You live in the <u>chieftain's</u> long house. You eat good food. You never think of the old days, but I do. They are never out of my mind."

"It is useless to think of them. They are gone. I will talk to Black Moccasin and perhaps he will take you into his lodge. I know he will."

"I do not wish to live in Black Moccasin's lodge."

"But how can you ever find your way home?"

"The people are hunting buffalo now. They will be near the place where we were captured. Remember how I left signs along the trail? I will find the signs."

Her mind was fixed. She was a true Shoshone. "I will not go. But I will help you. What do you want of me?"

"You can save food. Pemmican and smoked deermeat. Enough for ten sleeps."

"You will need more than ten."

"And a horse. One of Black Moccasin's horses."

I saved food for her, a little each day so as not to make the wives suspicious. The horse was more difficult. Black Moccasin's horses were kept in the lodge at night. At last she decided to take one in the daytime.

18

At dawn when the herd was driven to the river to drink, we followed it. While I talked to the herdsmen, Running Deer chose one of the best of the herd. She led it into a willow grove and disappeared.

The horse was not missed until nightfall. By then Running Deer was far out on the trail that would lead her home.

Chapter Five

The next day and the next I went around in my antelope clothes. With the purple dots on my cheeks and the vermilion-painted ears and the part in my hair, I went gracefully in my new moccasins that made a sound like the wind in the trees.

But Red Hawk took no notice of me, though I passed close to him many times.

One day, as I was coming back from the village spring, dressed now in my old clothes and with a jar of water balanced on my head, he stopped me. In a haughty way, as if he were not the son of Black Moccasin but the chieftain himself, he asked:

"Are you the girl I have seen?"

I was able to say, "You see many girls. I do not know if I am the girl you saw."

He was not pleased. "You carry water in a jar. You sit by the fire and stitch? You're the Shoshone, the one Tall Rock captured?"

"Yes."

"Do you speak Minnetaree?"

"Some. Not much."

"How much? I gave a speech in your hearing. What did I say?"

The truth was, I had not listened. Sitting in a strange place among strangers, my cheeks covered with purple dots and the inside of my ears painted crimson, on display before a man it seemed my fate to marry, I could not listen.

Red Hawk thought I was shy. He asked me again what I had heard. Since my childhood I had heard dozens of speeches by men back from the hunt, so I took pieces out of what I remembered and answered him.

He seemed pleased, but more with himself than with me. When I had finished, without a word he strode away.

After I reached the long house and emptied the water I was sent back for more. Now that summer had gone, the spring ran in driblets. Night was gathering by the time I filled the jar again. As I balanced the jar on my head, a hand reached out and touched my arm, a hand with a knife in it.

"Quiet," Tall Rock whispered.

I dropped the jar and started to run. The cold blade of the knife pressed against my back. I tried to scream but all that came out of my throat was a gasp.

"Quiet," Tall Rock said, pushing the knife. "You will not be hurt."

A horse was tied to a tree near the spring. Tall Rock lifted me to its back and slid up behind. He kept the knife against my back as we circled the village. Fires were burning in all the lodges but no one took notice except a dog that barked at us and followed at our heels to the northward trail.

Dark mist dripped from the trees. Tall Rock put his knife away and rode with his arms around me. His breath was hot on my neck.

"We go to Hidatsa, the village of the good Minnetarees, where I have friends," he said. It was the first warmth I had ever heard from him. "I know the chief of Hidatsa. He is my friend and not a friend of Black Moccasin. He will protect us. We will live in his big village forever."

I gripped the horse's mane and tried to calm myself.

21

The chieftain of Hidatsa was known and hated for his brutal deeds, even by his own tribe. His real name was Kakoakis, but behind his back he was called by a French name, Le Borgne. If a mother wished to scare a naughty child, all she need do was to say, "If you are not careful, the monster Le Borgne will get you."

There was no moon to see by and twice we got lost, so it was nightfall of the next day before we reached Hidatsa.

We went straight to Le Borgne's lodge, which was larger than the one I lived in. Its walls were hung with row upon row of scalps and other trophies.

Le Borgne was stretched out on a buffalo robe beside a fire, eating his supper. He stopped eating but did not move from his bed. He looked up at Tall Rock, then at me.

He was called Le Borgne because he had only one good eye; the other eye had something over it that looked like a little white curtain.

Tall Rock talked a long time about the good things he had heard about his friend, Kakoakis, and the chief's many exploits and how much the people in Hidatsa village loved him and how much he was feared and hated by Black Moccasin.

At last he came to his reason for being in the presence of the great chief of the Hidatsa Minnetarees, whom he called Kakoakis because he knew that the chieftain did not like the name One Eye, which many people called him behind his back.

"As you are aware," he said, "your enemy, Black Moccasin, is too ancient to take this girl for a wife. Instead, he has chosen a son to take his place."

"Red Hawk?" Le Borgne asked.

"The one who has a large bug in his head."

"Who talks about himself, even in his sleep."

"Ai," Tall Rock said. "Black Moccasin has no right to give her away to his son, and the son has no right to take her."

"No right," Le Borgne said in a high, thin voice that

22

sounded like the lash of a whip. "No right, because you captured the girl." He paused to gaze at me with his one good eye. "A pretty girl. A Shoshone?"

"Yes."

"I thought so from the look. Gentle people, but full of craziness if their pride is touched. One of my first wives was a Shoshone, long ago. I could not tame that one."

The first story I had heard when I went to live with the Minnetarees was about Le Borgne and the Shoshone girl—the one he had in a fit of rage scalped and killed.

"What do you wish from me?" he asked. "Speak, and it belongs to you."

"A place for us in your village. Away from Black Moccasin's wrath."

"You came on horses?"

"On one."

"Bring it," Le Borgne said, pointing to a corral in the far end of the lodge.

Tall Rock went to get the horse.

"How old are you?" Le Borgne asked me.

"Thirteen," I told him.

"Have you been married at some time?"

"No."

"Do you wish to marry this one?"

I hesitated, afraid to answer one way or the other. I was afraid of both men, of Le Borgne especially.

"You look frightened," he said, lifting himself to his feet. "You don't have to marry Tall Rock. You know this, daughter. I can send him away now, tonight. You will be safe here with Chief Kakoakis."

Tall Rock led the horse to the corral and came back to us with a long speech. Le Borgne paid no attention. His one eye passed over him and fixed itself on me.

Chapter Six

Le Borgne had food brought for us, and after I had eaten he called one of his wives, who showed me to a sleeping place. There was a bear rug to step on and a bed, not a pallet, raised off the floor as high as my knees.

I was so tired I did not try to sleep. I lay quiet, staring at the fire shadows. There was nothing to decide for I had already decided.

I waited until the two men went to bed and the fire died. I had taken off only my moccasins. I picked them up and made my way to the door.

Outside, I sat down and put on the moccasins, which took some time because they were wet and had shrunk. A narrow path led through the village and all the lodges faced it. I wanted to circle around behind them, but it was too dark, though a thin moon shone in the west.

Before I had gone far, dogs began to bark. Two of them followed me, growling at my heels. A short way beyond the village, I heard a shout and the sound of hoofs in the distance.

The country on both sides of the trail was open. There was no place to hide. I ran for a moment or two, hopelessly, fearing that I would be overtaken, for Metaharta was miles away.

The trail met the stream and followed along beside it. I thought of trying to hide in the water. Then I saw a row of bullboats pulled up on the shore. I chose the largest one, crawled inside, and sat down on the bottom.

Three horsemen rode by at a gallop. One of the horses, the spotted one, belonged to Tall Rock. I waited for a while. Then I lifted the boat into the stream and steered it close to the bank. The current took me toward my new home.

A short distance before it reaches the village, the river narrows and the current runs very fast. Minnetaree bullboats are very light, made of buffalo hide stretched on willow frames round as a ring. If you do not know how to handle them, they spin like feathers in the wind. I had seen them paddled but it was the first time I ever was in a Minnetaree bullboat.

It began to go round and round. I clawed hard with my paddle, to one side and then to the other, in front of me and behind, but still I spun in the fast water.

I passed my village, went on spinning for half a league, and at last spun into the broad Missouri. I was too happy to have escaped from Le Borgne and Tall Rock to be frightened.

In the slower current of the river the boat stopped spinning. I steered toward the west and for a while I thought I would reach shore. The boat caught on a snag, then floated safely away, but in the next two breaths, with an awful grating sound, struck something hard.

I found myself lying against a pile of driftwood, half in and half out of the river. My mouth was full of sand. The boat spun away in the night.

I lay there too exhausted to move. At daylight I crawled out of the water. I was on a small island with a wide stretch of brown water on both sides. The village of Metaharta was out of sight somewhere behind me.

The island was flat except for a large hillock in the center. I walked along the shore, which was littered with things washed down from above. It took me only a short time to circle the island, altogether about the same number of steps as if I made a circle of Black Moccasin's village.

I climbed the hillock and found cottonwood trees, nine of them, at the top, willows, two plum trees, a chokecherry tree, and a thicket of cactus pears. The view from here was the same as from below—a vast expanse of water, flat shores on both sides of the river, but no sign of life anywhere.

It was a good place to build a fire. I had to build one to keep warm. Also the rising smoke would let the people in Black Moccasin's village know that I was on the island. I wanted them to come and bring me back to the village.

I had no fear that Le Borgne or Tall Rock would see my fire from the high bluff on the east side of the river because the bluff and the land around it belonged to Black Moccasin. Le Borgne and Tall Rock would not dare to come there.

Two sandbars stretched out like arms at the head of the island. The river had run between them for a long time and left a great pile of driftwood on the shore. I gathered up an armful of dry branches, which I took to the hillock.

I had made many fires in my life, but this one was the hardest of all. I needed a knife to scrape up a pinch of dust. I only had a deer's shinbone. Instead of a stick, which I could twirl between my hands, I had to use the shinbone.

At last I got the dust to smoke. At last I coaxed out a pale spark. Finally, I blew the spark into a fire. By nightfall I had a fire that could be seen from far away.

I was not hungry and had no thought of eating, though there was some overripe fruit on the plum trees and green prickly pears in the thicket.

Near the fire I hollowed out a place where I was sheltered

26

by the cottonwoods, and I lay down and covered myself with leaves.

I watched the stars move across the sky. I listened through the night for the sound of a boat on the river. From time to time I got up and put fresh branches on the fire. No one came. All I heard was the whimpering of nighthawks.

I fed the fire throughout the day. While it burned and smoke trailed away on the cold wind, I went off looking for food that could be smoked over the fire.

I circled the island and saw shoals of small silver fish and one big fish, half as big as I was, black on top and white underneath, with yellow eyes and long feelers on each side of its mouth. It was friendly, letting me get within arm's length. I had caught river fish often in Shoshone country, being very patient, putting out a hand slowly, then clamping down, but this one backed away and disappeared in the dark water.

I thought there might be squirrels in the thicket, possibly rabbits. I found nothing except three prairie dog burrows. Each held a store of good roots, but since the roots were their food for a long winter I did not take them.

I still believed that my fire would be seen at night, or the smoke in the daytime, by someone passing along the bluffs.

After these two days when I had little to eat, I built a weir out of willow branches at the place where the river met the island. But the current was too strong and sent the weir floating away.

It was at dusk when this happened. I felt like weeping, but as I watched the weir float down the river, I looked up and saw the Evening Star sparkling in the west. The star was my talisman. It was the sign the Great Spirit had given me when I was only a child to guide and protect me forever.

The Spirit had given it to me in this way and for this reason. It was the summer of my sixth year and our tribe was camped where the three rivers meet. I was too young to know a friend from an enemy. To me, all people were alike.

27

My family was sitting by the fire in our tipi talking. I was eating from a bowl of soup and had a spoonful to my mouth when I saw the shadow of someone standing near the doorway. I got up and went to the door and held out a spoonful of soup for the shadow to eat.

The shadow belonged to an enemy, a Blackfoot chief. He drank the soup, then went back to his warriors, who had surrounded our camp, and told them he did not wish to attack us.

The next morning I found a green stone shaped like the Evening Star lying in the grass where the chieftain had been. This stone I have worn ever since and have never taken it off.

At dusk of my fourth day on the island, while I collected wood for the fire, I came upon the carcass of a deer deep in the driftwood. From the four arrows stuck in its back, I guessed that the wounded beast had fled into the river to escape the hunters, only to be swept to its death.

The flesh was rank but when I smoked it the taste was good. I had no way of making a bow, which was disappointing, but the arrow tips were metal and the wrappings were well-cured leather.

I made a short fishline from the wrappings and a hook from the metal, and I baited the hook with a piece of the deermeat. I caught a string, as long as my arm, of the silver fish. These I smoked over the fire and hung in the cottonwood trees, with pieces of copper twirling in the wind to keep the ravens away. From the deer's hide, using an arrow tip to scrape it clean, I made a rough cape for myself.

All of this good fortune was a gift from my talisman, the star that comes out at nightfall.

Chapter Seven

I kept my fire burning night and day. I saw figures moving along the high bluff but no one came.

The nights grew colder. The wind shifted to the north and stayed there. <u>Torrents</u> of geese began to pour down from the north. A few stopped to rest on the island, but I had no way of catching them. I ate the last of the deermeat and half of my smoked fish. Still no one came to look for me.

I thought of making a raft out of logs, lashing them together with strips taken from my deerskin cape. There was not enough leather to do this the right way, so I thought of getting a log and drifting downstream until I reached land on one side or the other. I gave this idea up because the current was strong, and if I drifted south for no longer than a day, I would be deep in the country of our enemies, the marauding Sioux.

The nights grew bitter cold. Cakes of ice floated past and some piled up at the head of the island. A thin crust froze along the riverbank. It was possible that the whole river would freeze over. If it did, then I could cross over to the far shore.

It was too cold to sleep on the ground in a hollow covered only by a blanket of leaves. I put up a lean-to of driftwood against the trunk of the largest of the cottonwoods, covered it with willow branches, and dug a deep pit for the fire close to the doorway.

I caught another small string of fish and smoked them. But whatever I was doing I stopped to scan the shores to the east and the west. At nightfall I watched the Evening Star and spoke to her.

Ice was growing thick along the banks. Cakes of ice floated past now in a steady stream. Some of them were half the size of my island. On one of the cakes were two deer. I watched them go past without feeling sad, for if they had piled up onshore, I had no way of killing them.

It rained and the rain turned to sleet. The sleet turned to snow. The sun came out in a stormy sky. Through the pale light I saw on a cake of ice what I thought was a brown bear sitting on its haunches. As the ice floated closer, dipping from one side to the other under the beast's weight, I saw that it was not a bear but a buffalo cow.

The ice cake brushed the shore. It was dipping away, back into the current, when the beast plunged into the water, climbed the bank, and stood staring at me. Buffalo are gentle beasts if not wounded. I stared back at her and she moved away toward the far end of the island.

It snowed in the night. When I got up to put wood on the fire and cook a fish for breakfast, I saw hoofmarks in the snow. They made circles, many of them, around the hillock. The cow had seen the cottonwoods and wanted to eat their bark but was afraid to come closer.

I broke off some of the cottonwood branches and went to find her. She stood by the pile of driftwood, trying to find bark she could eat among the barkless logs. I came close to her and held out the cottonwood branches. She moved away from me, so I left the food and went back to finish my breakfast.

She was at the same place the next morning. I left food for her again, but after that, since it was a long walk in the icy air, each day I left food for her closer and closer to the hillock.

Each day I tried to get her to eat from my hand. And always she backed away, though not as quickly, her head lowered and her yellow eyes fixed upon me without so much as a single blink.

I got tired of her ways. I thought, what a fine warm robe you would make, and that big long tongue of yours, which you slurp up food with, would be very good roasted on the fire.

Soon she began taking food from my hand and each morning I found her at the door of my lean-to. The cottonwoods, the big grove of willows, and the thicket of prickly pears were nearby, but she much preferred that I feed her. I liked this. She was good company. She kept me from thinking about myself.

The river was frozen over now on both sides of the island except for channels down the center. The channels were too wide to swim across.

My food ran low. Thinking about it, I remembered the winter when food ran out and all the Shoshones had to eat bark from the trees. Some ate their moccasins, though I never did. Now from time to time I feared that I might have to.

One morning, after it had snowed all night, I went out to the west bank of the island. There was a white glare on the ice and the river that blinded me, but I was sure I saw a canoe coming toward me from the south, against the current.

There were two people in the canoe, both of them paddling. I took off my cape and waved it, fearing that in the icy glare they would miss me.

The one in the back of the canoe raised his hand to let me

know that he saw me. Then he turned toward the bank where I stood. A girl in the front of the canoe held out her paddle and I grasped the end of it and pulled them in.

The man got up, stretched himself, and stepped onshore. Huge, bigger than Le Borgne but not tall, he was wrapped in a bearskin cape and wore a red fox cap with the fluffy tail dangling behind. I could see only his eyes, which were set close to his nose and looked like small, dark pebbles.

He made signs with his mittened hands. He asked me what tribe I belonged to. When I pointed toward the village, he smiled.

"Metaharta?"

I nodded.

He did not ask me why I was on an island in the middle of the river in the wintertime.

"I go there," he said in Minnetaree. "You want to come?"

"Yes."

"Now?"

"Now."

"Get in," he said, holding the canoe for me.

The buffalo cow stood a short distance away, looking at us. The man asked the girl to hand him his firestick. He put it to his shoulder. Fire came out the end, then a lot of smoke.

When the smoke drifted away, the cow was lying on her side. With a sharp knife he butchered the carcass and he gave the pieces to the girl, who put them in a neat pile.

Sweating in the bitter cold, he pulled the robe away from his face. It was covered with hair, right up to his eyes. Never had I seen a man with a hairy face before. He did not belong to our people. Our people were without hair. If the smallest hair did appear, our men plucked it out with deerbone tweezers.

The man wiped his face on his arm and, with the firestick

between his knees, took up his paddle and started across the river.

The girl was very young. She paddled with the same stroke he used, as though they had traveled much together. Once she paused and turned to look at me. I smiled and she smiled back. It was not a friendly smile. Her name was Otter Woman.

meeting Charbon.

Chapter Eight

The Minnetarees ran to the shore when news spread that a white trader had come. They swarmed around our big canoe. They pointed to the trader's piles of meat and his trading goods. Musicians with drums and rattles and turkeybone whistles marched the trader to the council ground. Otter Woman and I trailed along behind.

They built a great fire in front of the long house and danced. Black Moccasin spoke a welcome. He said many good things about the man who had brought me home to the village. His name was Toussaint Charbonneau. Black Moccasin called him "the Frenchman."

All during the talk Charbonneau clung to my arm as though he was afraid I might run away. Red Hawk stood beside his father and did not listen to the talk. His eyes were fixed on Charbonneau.

Red Hawk left and went into the lodge. As the talk ended, he swaggered out and stood beside his father. He had changed his clothes. Before he had worn a breechcloth and a coyote skin thrown over his shoulders. Now he was dressed in a beaded robe, a necklace of bear claws, and leggings decorated with porcupine quills.

The moment his father's talk came to an end, Red Hawk pushed himself between Charbonneau and me. It was a hostile act. The Frenchman backed away. He stood facing Red Hawk, his shaggy head lowered, his huge shoulders bent forward. The firelight shone in his eyes. He looked like a wounded bear.

Black Moccasin silenced both of the men with a sharp command. He grasped my arm, led me through the crowd into the lodge, sat me down by the fire, and threw a buffalo robe over my shoulders. He asked what had happened to me during the long time I had been gone. And when I told him, he was not troubled about either Tall Rock or Le Borgne, only about Toussaint Charbonneau. claim on Sac

"You saw him on the river," he said. "Did you call to him?"

"I waved my cape."

"But you did not cry out or act as though you were in danger."

"No."

"Did you ask him to bring you here?"

"No, he asked me if I wanted to go to the village and I said yes."

I knew what Black Moccasin was thinking. If the Frenchman had saved me from danger or captured me from an enemy, then, by the law of all the tribes, I belonged to Toussaint Charbonneau. To do with as he pleased.

"You are to marry my son Red Hawk," Black Moccasin said. "That is settled. That is decreed. It does not matter what the Frenchman thinks or wishes. He will not harm you. He thinks too much of the trades he makes with us. Nor will he run off with you as Tall Rock did."

Black Moccasin poked the fire with his walking stick and waited for me to say something.

I was too confused to say a word. I should have said, "I do not like Red Hawk and I do not think I will be happy with him. And if I am unhappy, then he will be unhappy too." But these words from a slave girl, not yet fourteen, to the chieftain of the Minnetarees, would have a foolish sound. In truth, I should have jumped up and run in rings. A Shoshone, a slave, a captive, to marry the son of the great chieftain. How fortunate I was!

"I see you are troubled," he said. "Even my old ears can hear your heart beat. Calm yourself. Stay in the lodge. Do not go out for any reason, not until the Frenchman leaves."

"Why?"

"He says one thing and means another."

"You do not trust him?"

"No, he is half white and half Sioux."

"When will he go?"

"Before the next moon. Then he goes to trade with One Eye. One Eye does not like to have us pick things over too much."

Black Moccasin called his wives and told them to give me food, to put me to bed, and to keep me there until the sun came on another day. "Then see that she has something to do. She is not to go into the village."

I followed him to the doorway and looked out. The council place overflowed with people. The pitchwood fire burned high and sent black clouds spinning in the air. Toussaint Charbonneau and the girl were dancing, a dance I had never seen before. They hopped around like frogs.

"It's the white man's dance," Black Moccasin said. "They dance because of the whiskey that builds a fire in their bellies. Not to the sun, not to the moon, not to the Great Spirit below us, above us, around us everywhere."

The Frenchman stopped dancing. He upended a leather bag and drank from it.

"There is a thing I do not understand," I said. "You have told me that Charbonneau will not harm me. Yet I must stay here in the lodge until he leaves. I have been away from my friends for a long time. I would like to talk to them."

Black Moccasin frowned. He was not used to having a girl question him.

Patiently, he said, "The Frenchman will not harm you for it would mean his death. But if you walk in the village it is sure to cause trouble between him and my son. Or bad feelings. And I do not want bad feelings. I want Charbonneau to come back. My people like to trade with him. If you are out of sight he will forget you. He has forgotten many girls along this river and other rivers, too."

Charbonneau was dancing again, this time with Lightning in Her Hair, one of my friends, the prettiest girl among all the Minnetarees.

I watched Charbonneau leap about with Lightning in Her Hair. She leaped too. She seemed to be happy. The fire glistened on his hairy face. He still looked like a wounded bear.

"Gladly will I sit in the lodge. I do not wish to see this man again," I said to myself.

The Frenchman traded all the next day. The wives of Black Moccasin came back from the trading place with a shiny knife, an iron kettle to cook in, three long sewing needles, and a length of pink goods, enough to make four dresses.

There was no word from the Frenchman himself. But the women said that he was in a happy mood. He joked with everyone, took long drinks from his leather jug, and sang songs they did not understand. But he did not say a word about me.

Word came later, the next day at noon. It was brought by Black Moccasin. I could see that it was bad when he sat down beside the fire.

"You are not to blame us if things go wrong," he said. "If you have to marry Toussaint Charbonneau and not my son."

I was sewing on a deerskin robe. I stopped sewing to stare at him.

37

"The Frenchman went into a rage when he heard that you and Red Hawk were to be married. He took a knife from his belt and stormed around, threatening everyone in the village. He stormed at me. I told him that the marriage was decreed long before he came. He said that you were near death from the winter cold when he rescued you. He asked me why I had not gone out to search for you, why no one had rescued you."

I jumped to my feet. "I was not dying when he found me. I had shelter and fire and food. In a very short time the river would have frozen over and I could have walked to the shore."

"This is true as you say it, but to him it is not true. To him you were saved from death. Therefore you are his, the same as if he had found a wounded beast with arrows in it."

"Not the same," I said. "When the Frenchman found me, I was not a wounded beast. Nor am I a wounded beast now."

Black Moccasin gave me a straight look. He was displeased that his judgment was questioned, that I dared speak in such a voice. I had a strong feeling that my fate had already been decided. I was to marry the Frenchman no matter what my feelings were.

Not only did an honorable law demand it. Charbonneau was a trader whose friendship was very important to the tribe. He must not leave the village an angry man who felt that he had been treated poorly.

"Smile," Black Moccasin said. "I will smile too. A plan of mine may work. Have you played the Hand Game?"

"Yes, Shoshone children play it."

"It is not played in Metaharta for fun, only to settle arguments, such as what arrow of many arrows has killed a buffalo. Three will play the game. Toussaint Charbonneau and Red Hawk and Le Borgne all claim you."

"Le Borgne?" I said, surprised. "Why does he claim me?"

38

"He says that he took you away from the scoundrel Tall Rock and protected you. He says that you ran away and hid. In his village of Hidatsa this is a crime. The punishment is death. From all that you told me, you did run from him and hide."

"Le Borgne is a brute. I have heard you say it. Why must you listen to him?"

"Because he rules a village more powerful than mine. I cannot stand against One Eye and his village, which is bigger than Metaharta by two times."

My heart stopped beating. "If Red Hawk loses the game, then I belong to either Charbonneau or Le Borgne?"

"That is the rule. There is no other. But Red Hawk will not lose. He never loses. He always wins."

My heart started to beat again. "Why does Red Hawk never lose?"

"Because he always receives help from the Great Spirit who guards our village. The Spirit helps him to see through flesh and bone, through the closed hands of those he plays against. Into the palm of their hands. He can see, as clear as if it lay right there beside the fire, what is in the hands. Who holds the plum seed that is carved with the sign of the moon or the seed that is uncarved."

"Do the Frenchman and Le Borgne know that Red Hawk never loses?"

"If they did know, they would not play."

"When does the game start?"

"Tonight is the best time for Red Hawk. His spirit sees better in the dark than in the light. He never loses when the game is played in the dark. Tonight is the night he will play because the moon will cast shadows."

When Black Moccasin left me, I got ready to speak to my talisman. I could not go into the village and find a quiet place. I could not see her in the sky now. But she was there waiting for the night to come. I went and lay beside my bed and waited.

39

Chapter Nine

Night came slowly. I looked up through the hole in the roof and saw night shadows and the first faint star. Black Moccasin sent for me. His wives had built a fire of willow branches and he sat beside it in his heavy bear cape.

"Find a place where you can see and not be seen," he said to Blue Sky. "Sacagawea should not be here at all, but better here than somewhere else. Stand her on the other side of the fire, where you can keep an eye on her. If the game goes bad, if she is tempted to flee, be ready to stop her."

Against all the laws, Minnetaree laws and Shoshone laws, I spoke up. "You said that your son Red Hawk never loses in the Game of Hands."

"So I did. And now I say it again. Red Hawk never loses in the Game of Hands." He gave me a sharp look and said to his wife, "Take the girl away. Guests clamor at the gate."

The beat of drums and loud voices came from outside. A gust of wind swept the lodge as Toussaint Charbonneau burst in, followed by Le Borgne and his followers. Black Moccasin pointed to the blanket spread in front of him and bade the men to take their places.

Le Borgne and his followers, whose cheeks were painted

40

with dots and swirls, sat at one end of the blanket. Charbonneau sat at the other end. I could not see his face because of the hair that covered it and hung down over his chest like a black curtain. Red Hawk came. He smiled to himself and sat in the middle.

"Red Hawk looks happy," I said.

"He talks to the Great Spirit," his mother explained.

"Is the Great Spirit listening?" I asked.

"He always listens to Red Hawk."

The other wives began to sing and all twelve children joined in with deerbone rattles. At the same time loud chanting came from the warriors gathered outside. In the awful din, Black Moccasin tried to explain the rules.

They were the same as those in the place I was born, only here plum seeds were used instead of bones. One of the seeds was rubbed smooth and the other had a small dent in it, colored yellow and blue.

The game was simple. Each player tried to hide the dented pit. He could stand and move his hands and body any way he chose, but not his feet. When he was done with his movements and put his tight fists on the blanket, one of those playing against him must choose the hand that held the colored plum pit.

The score was kept by the chieftain and the winner was the one who guessed right four times, the mystical number of all the tribes.

Charbonneau passed a jug of rum. Le Borgne drank but Red Hawk refused. He got to his knees, took the two plum pits from his father, and tossed them into the air. He caught them in one hand, clasped his hands together, and made the pits rattle. Then he put his fists on the blanket in front of Charbonneau.

The Frenchman reached out two long thumbs and pressed hard on each of the fists. He was trying to find the hidden seed.

"You have played this game before?" Red Hawk asked him.

"Often," Charbonneau said. "More often than Red Hawk, among many peoples."

"If you know so much, Charbonneau, do not press so hard or you will crush the seeds."

Charbonneau said nothing and took his thumbs away. His narrow head thrust out. He peered at the clenched hands. "Her," he said, pointing.

Red Hawk turned his fist over, taking his time. He showed an empty palm.

"Zut!" the Frenchman shouted. He took a drink from the jug and wiped his mouth on the kerchief around his neck. "The other hand, let me see her, huh?"

Red Hawk opened his fist and Charbonneau saw that it held two plum seeds. He rubbed his eyes, grabbed the seeds, and jumped to his feet. He raised his hands over his head, yelled like a coyote, and quacked like a duck. Then he shoved his hands close to Le Borgne's beaked nose.

The great chieftain of the Hidatsa Minnetarees closed the eye he could see from. He kept the other eye open and chose the hand that held the colored plum seed.

A warrior was sitting on the roof, watching through the smoke hole. He shouted down to the warriors at the gate that their great chieftain had won.

The chanting grew louder, but Le Borgne only smirked. From the moment he strode into the lodge he had shown that it hurt his pride to play a game to win a girl, a slave girl who by all rights belonged to him already.

I must have gasped as he twisted his mouth, for Blue Sky said quickly, "The Great Spirit does not like the man. He can never win the game."

"But if he does?"

"I will go with you and take you home to the Shoshone," she said, "and he will never find you."

Le Borgne picked up the plum seeds carefully, one at a

42

time, as if they were hot stones. He did not bother to shake them. He did open his hands up near his eye and for a long time looked at them.

"Choose," he said to Red Hawk. "And do not move the feet like the Frenchman, who acts like a buffalo with ten arrows stuck in him. It is against the rules to move the feet."

Red Hawk guessed at once and chose the right hand, the one that held the colored seed. At this, the singing of the wives grew louder and the children rattled their deerbones and danced around. Red Hawk looked to make sure that I had seen. I gave a sign and smiled. He did not smile back at me.

His mother said, "He thinks well of you. But now his mind is with the game. He cannot smile until the game is over."

The wind, chasing its windy tail, roared around the lodge. Some of it roared down the smoke hole, so Black Moccasin sent one of his wives up on the roof to cover it with a blanket.

Charbonneau won the next game and the next. Le Borgne won the following game.

Black Moccasin kept the score, which stood two for Charbonneau, two for Le Borgne, and one for Red Hawk. It was the Frenchman's turn now.

As before, he went through all of his antics. He also added new ones. He sat on his hands and howled like a wolf and bellowed like a bull buffalo.

Red Hawk groaned while all this was going on. When it was over and Charbonneau held out his hands for him to choose, he said, "Nothing is left of the plum seeds. You have worn them out, Frenchman."

Surely the words were a joke, but Charbonneau did not take them that way. He glared at Red Hawk and fingered the knife in his belt. For a moment I thought he meant to use it. Instead, he shouted, "Choose! No more talk. Talk gives Charbonneau bugs in the ear."

"He has a big temper, this Frenchman," Blue Sky said. "Sometime it will give him more than bugs. It will give him big trouble."

Red Hawk waited, seeking the colored seed, talking to himself.

My heart beat in my throat. Blue Sky must have heard it for she put an arm around me. "He talks to the Great Spirit. He will choose wisely," she said.

But Red Hawk did not choose wisely.

Then the game went fast. Le Borgne took the plum pits and lost to Toussaint Charbonneau. It was Red Hawk's turn again and Charbonneau needed only one good guess to win.

Raising his hands, Red Hawk drew them far apart, but as he brought them together one of the seeds slipped away and fell on the blanket. It is a bad omen, I thought to myself, and Blue Sky thought so too. Her arm grew tight around me.

"Your hands fly like goose," Charbonneau said, passing his jug to Red Hawk. "Here, drink! Drink, friend, huh?"

Red Hawk had not touched the jug before when it was offered to him. Now he drank deep, drank a second time, and passed the jug back to the Frenchman, who put it down without drinking.

"This is foolish," Blue Sky said. "I do not like it."

The blanket had blown off the smoke hole, and cold, hissing gusts of air swooped down. The wives brought armfuls of buffalo chips and heaped them on the fire. They smoked so much that it was hard to see what Red Hawk was doing.

He was on his feet. He was swaying from side to side, holding the plum seeds above his head. Then he twisted them around, the way the Frenchman had done, around his knees and between them.

Blue Sky gasped. She took her hand from my shoulder and held it over her mouth. The singing had stopped. There were no sounds from outside except from the man who was

44

at the smoke hole again, shouting down to those who stood at the gate.

In the midst of everything, Great Chief Le Borgne rose with a bow to Black Moccasin and silently left the lodge. He slammed the door behind him. For a while shouts echoed and rocks were hurled against the door and fell upon the roof.

Charbonneau stared at me, shielding his eyes against the glare of the fire. It was hard to tell with all the hair he wore on his face, but I thought I saw his lips move in a smile. I did not smile back.

It was very quiet as Red Hawk drew himself together, closed his hands, and put them on the blanket in front of Charbonneau. The Frenchman gave them a sidelong glance. He shielded his eyes again and looked at me, to make sure I was watching.

With a flourish, he put a thumb on the right hand. When it did not open, he pried it open with big paws. In Red Hawk's hand he found the colored seed.

Charbonneau heaved to his feet and stretched himself. His hairy face loomed through the smoke.

Blue Sky took my arm. "I will be slow to give you up," she said, leading me away.

Chapter Ten

Charbonneau came to the lodge soon after dawn to take me away. Snow was falling and the wind blew, but Blue Sky made him wait at the door until we had eaten. When she let him in, he did not want to talk to her and asked for Black Moccasin.

"He sleeps," Blue Sky said.

"I wait," Charbonneau said.

"Sometimes he sleeps all day."

"I wait."

"In the winter he sleeps sometimes for two days. What do you want of him?"

"That girl," he said, pointing at me.

Last night he was angry when she took me away and he was angry now, though he spoke soft words.

"Winter is here," she said. "Go trade with Le Borgne. Come back when the snows are gone. Then you can build a lodge and have a proper place to keep your wives."

"Charbonneau trades," he said. "Charbonneau does not build tipis or wigwams or wickiups or hogans. He go trade one village to another village. On river and far from river. He takes journeys. You see?"

"I see," said Blue Sky. "That is why I tell you to come back when there are no more snows."

His black eyes snapped. "Talk? Why talk? This girl she belong to Toussaint Charbonneau. This girl . . . What is the name of this girl, anyway?"

"Sacagawea."

"Sacagawea? What does this word mean?"

"Bird Girl. Bird Woman."

"Huh," Charbonneau grunted. "Bird Girl better. No like bird woman. Like bird girls."

We were in the lodge, huddled at the fire. Black Moccasin came and sat down. Usually Blue Sky made decisions for the family. Black Moccasin was happy not to be bothered, but he did speak up now.

"Enough, Charbonneau," he said. "Go. We will talk again when spring comes."

Charbonneau stood over the old chieftain. He fingered his hunting knife. As long as I knew him, he always fingered it when he was angry. The old man gave back to him a sullen gaze.

I did not want to marry Toussaint Charbonneau. He scared me. The locks of lank hair, the black beard, the tufts of black hair on his hands, the huge shoulders, the lumbering gait, always reminded me of a buffalo or a bear.

I told this to Blue Sky on the day that Charbonneau came back from the villages far up the river.

Soon afterward she said to him, "While you were gone we built a fine lodge for you and your wives. It is built of antelope skins and has two bearskins on the floor. It is big, big enough for a big family."

"I do not wish the lodge. Charbonneau goes down river. He goes to great city, St. Louis. He trades with Sioux and Iowas, also Kickapoos. Charbonneau goes north also. He trades with Dakotas and Ojibways and Assiniboins. Charbonneau travels much. Charbonneau does not sit in lodge."

"You don't need to sit," Blue Sky said. "You go south,

north, in every direction, but this wife stays safe in the lodge while you are away. She will make a home for you in the village of Metaharta."

He raised his hands above his head. He clutched his hair and pulled at it in a frenzy. "Charbonneau," he said, "do not wish to come home to wives. He wishes wives with him where he go."

"You trade with the Sioux, our enemies," she said. "With our enemies the Assiniboins, also. You cannot take this girl among our enemies unless she wishes to go."

Blue Sky turned to me for an answer.

She read it in my eyes. The fear of danger and even death among hostile tribes for me and the children I might bear. My strong feelings for my new home and friends—how sad it would be to leave them! The fear of marriage to a man I scarcely knew. All was there in my eyes for her to see.

She said to Charbonneau, "You have a right to Sacagawea. You won her in the game. So you can marry her, but you cannot take her from the village."

Charbonneau started to tear his hair again.

"I have spoken," Blue Sky said. "I speak these words for Black Moccasin and for myself."

Charbonneau must have seen in one quick glance that he could never hope to stand against this woman. He quit tearing at his hair and tried to smile.

"When does marriage happen?" he stammered. "Now, good for Toussaint Charbonneau."

"Six suns from now," said Blue Sky.

"Not good."

"Six," Blue Sky said.

Charbonneau suddenly reached for me, but I drew away fast. We left him standing there. He bellowed after us in angry French words and Minnetaree. Blue Sky did not look back or heed him.

"This Charbonneau," she said, when we were inside the lodge, "is a wild animal that needs taming. You cannot

48

tame him by yourself, so I will help you. Long ago, Black Moccasin was wild, too, though never wild like this one. Look at Black Moccasin now, how gentle he is. Yes, I need to help you."

"Hide me until he has gone," I begged her. "He will be gone for many suns. In that time he will forget and find another girl that pleases him."

Blue Sky shook her head. "He will cause much trouble. Much for you and much for all of us. He has fixed his mind on you. He will not forget."

"I can hide myself. I can flee."

"Charbonneau will find you, wherever you go. If you were his wife and fled, then he has the right by our laws to kill you. You are not his wife. You are a slave, but still he can punish you. True Arrow, one of our chiefs, owned a slave woman and she fled and when he caught her he cropped both her ears and the tip of her nose. That is the law of the Minnetarees."

"Charbonneau is not a Minnetaree."

"But you are a Minnetaree," Blue Sky said. She took my hand. "Make a good home for him. If he does not like the home you make, then you can rid yourself of Toussaint Charbonneau. Phut."

Chapter Eleven

It did not take long for the wedding, not as it did at home. At home when my brother Cameahwait was married, it took two moons just to get ready.

It was this way. My brother talked to my father and told him that he wished to be married. My father thought Cameahwait was old enough to think straight, so he said, "Go and get married." But this did not happen right away.

First, my mother and father went to talk to the family of the girl my brother had chosen. They took nice presents— an antelope blanket, a tanned buffalo hide, and a white horse with a saddle. But they did not give the presents to the family at once. So that it would be a surprise, they left them outside for the family to find after they had gone.

They talked to the girl's mother and father for a long time. Just before they left they said that their son wished to marry.

This was good, her family said.

And then they told the girl about everything. Since she had been sitting in the tipi all this time, she had made up her mind already. Had she not liked my brother, her family would have given the presents back.

But she did like him.

So for days her family gathered up presents of their own, better than the ones they had received, such as two horses instead of one, and the girl put on her finest clothes and they all rode off to our tipi. My sister and I went out to greet them and my father and mother took the girl inside.

From that moment she was married to my brother.

There were no meetings about me and Toussaint Charbonneau. No friendly talks and no nice presents from one family to another.

As Blue Sky had decreed, Toussaint Charbonneau and I were married six days later, before a fire in the lodge she had built for us. She was at the wedding, but Red Hawk and Black Moccasin were not.

Charbonneau's first wife had a pot of deermeat cooking over the fire. She served it with squamash roots cooked in the ashes and a hot drink that tasted like honey. While she passed these things around, she smiled a lot, though she must have been unhappy.

She was not unhappy for long. Two days later she and Charbonneau left to trade at Le Borgne's village. I helped carry her things down to the canoe.

Charbonneau picked me up and whirled me around like a doll. "You careful now. You careful tomorrow too," he said and rubbed his hairy face against my cheek.

Otter Woman shyly touched me. In signs she made me see what she thought. She thought it was better to have a half part in a good man than a full part in a bad man.

I watched them go up the river. I felt nothing.

The next day Blue Sky asked me to come to the lodge and live there while they were gone. "It is warm in the lodge," she said. "You will not cook just for yourself and eat alone. You will have company. Alone the nights are long."

"I will come every day and eat."

I was only making a joke with her. I had married Toussaint Charbonneau. By the laws of the Minnetarees, I

51

was his wife. It was a burden set down upon my shoulders by my Guardian Spirit. It was placed there against my will and all my wishes. Yet the burden was mine.

I had a big supply of wood for a fire and dried meat and corn for food, also four deerskins and a long piece of sinew. I spent the days making a pair of moccasins and a mantle to take the place of the one I had worn out. The moccasins were useful when I had to go out to see Blue Sky.

I told her what was happening to me, how different I felt sometimes. She made me lie down on her bed. She felt my stomach up and down, round and round. She laughed.

"You will be a mother one of these times," she said.

"When?"

"Soon enough."

"When the snow comes?"

"After."

"How much?" I asked, beginning to shake.

"This many moons," she said and held up a lot of fingers.

"What shall I do?"

"You go and get your things and bring them here and sit down and make clothes for the baby. You will need a cradle too, but that can wait until we find a cedar tree to cut down. Bois d'arc is a good wood also, but it does not grow on the river."

I wanted to stay in my place, where I had been living happily enough, but Blue Sky made me move back to the big lodge. I moved that day. By nightfall she had me sorting out squirrel skins to make a blanket.

A few suns later, two men brought a small cedar, which they split into three pieces for me to work on. I had never made a baby's cradle or watched someone else make one, so Blue Sky had to show me how.

She gave me a sharp knife that she had got from Charbonneau one time and set me to whittling the boards, which were the length of my arms and the span of one hand in width. Cedar is a soft wood to touch, yet it is strong. My whittling dragged along, though the knife was sharp, and she made me throw away one of the pieces.

"It looks fine to me," I protested.

"To me it looks crooked," she said. "It will make a crooked cradle and a child with crooked legs."

"When I lived in a cradle," I told her, "it was just a tube of buffalo hide. I liked it very much. I liked it so much that when my mother took me out I always cried."

Blue Sky said, "There will be many moons before you need the cradle. Work on other things for your baby—a squirrel blanket, moccasins with fur on the inside, two plain, two with feathers for dress-up, a cap that pulls down over the ears, and a deerbone rattle. Big so it cannot be swallowed, only chewed upon."

I was ashamed, but I did not take her advice. Stubbornly, I went on with the cradle. I threw away the crooked piece and whittled a good one. When I had three shapely pieces, I bent a curved piece of tough hide across the tops, holding them tightly together. I made a bag of soft deerskin and stretched it down over the curved hide and the three pieces of cedar and tied it at the bottom. I lined the cradle with soft rabbit fur.

"Good!" Blue Sky said, holding the cradle up and turning it around. "The rawhide hood at the top is curved well. It is also strong. If the cradle falls when you hang it up, it will roll around on the ground."

I did not need her advice for the decorations. I had made all kinds of decorations when I was a child.

She gave me a bag of porcupine quills. I chose four of the longest and soaked them in water from one day to the next. I put them between my front teeth, clamped down hard, and pulled them flat as a ribbon. These I sewed on the hood of the cradle, two on one side and two on the other. Between the four black and white quills I painted a picture of the Evening Star with white clouds.

"Beautiful," Blue Sky said. "It's an omen. You will have a beautiful child. You are beautiful and Toussaint Charbonneau is ugly, but still you'll have a beautiful child."

"When?"

"Soon."

"Will my Guardian Spirit tell me when?"

"Yes. She will speak loudly in your ear. In both of your ears. She will speak to you in a clear voice. It is not an ache in the head. It is not a pain in the tooth, this child thing."

"What will Toussaint Charbonneau say when he comes back and sees me walking around fat?"

"If I know this man, he will stare at you, pull at that hair on his chin, and grunt. He will say, 'How can Charbonneau go trading up and down the river with a baby in a cradleboard hanging by his wife's neck?'"

Her words came true. When he did come back late in the autumn, that is what he did and what he said to me. He also said more. We were in the lodge and Blue Sky was helping me make another pair of moccasins, these of soft antelope skin.

He stared at me. He shook his head. He squinted through his locks of hair. "Charbonneau go far," he said. "Big town, St. Louis. Sell much. Buy much. Come here. See boy. Ai, ai!"

"A girl maybe," Blue Sky said. "A pretty one."

"Pretty girl, ugly girl—both bad," Charbonneau said. "Boy, name Jean Baptiste."

Otter Woman said, "Call him Brave Raven. My father's name is Brave Raven."

He gave her a hard look and said, "Jean Baptiste Charbonneau."

Chapter Twelve

When Charbonneau and Otter Woman came back, a man and a woman came with them. The man told us that his name was René Jessaume. Charbonneau told us that Jessaume was truthful and for us to believe what he was going to tell us.

Jessaume spoke in Minnetaree mixed up with a language I did not understand, which might have been Assiniboin. I could not make out much of what he said. I did learn that many white men were paddling up the river from the town called St. Louis in boats. One of them was half as long as Black Moccasin's long house.

Everyone held their breath until he was through his talk. Then they all talked at once and asked questions. Jessaume shrugged and said he knew nothing more.

Charbonneau counted the number of white men who were on the big boat coming up the river. He held up both his hands three times, then only one hand. "Friends. Fine mens," he said.

Black Moccasin had a fire built on the cliff in front of the village, where it could be seen from the river. The fire was kept burning. Watchers stood beside it and watched for the white men in the boats. They came on the day the first wild geese flew out of the north.

Watchers gave the news and all of us ran to the cliff. The big boat that Jessaume had told us about was within sight. As we watched, it slowly took shape and came out of the river mist. It looked like a great floating bird, with its sails spread out like silver wings. Jessaume called it a keelboat.

S. mile [margin annotation]

Red Hawk wanted the women to stay where they were on the cliff. Black Moccasin overruled his son. He started down with a band of warriors, taking bags of corn and dried deermeat, and motioned to us to follow him.

The boat was filled with white men. I had seen one of the whites, René Jessaume, but here was a crowd of them. They were young men in buffalo leather and with hairy faces. What skin you could see was dark from the sun.

They looked something like Minnetarees, except for one of them, who seemed to be a leader. At least he talked a lot and the rest of them listened. This one had blue eyes and hair as bright as copper.

Our chieftain welcomed him to the village of Metaharta. He pointed to himself and said, "Black Moccasin."

The man with the red hair smiled and bowed. "Clark," he said, pointing to himself. Then he pointed to a man beside him and said, "Captain Lewis."

This man bowed but he did not smile. It was the other one I liked, the man with the hair that shone like copper. He must have liked me too. He kept glancing at me while he talked to a man who was translating what he said, a man whose name was Drewyer.

Afterward Captain Clark came to where I stood on the bank and gave me four blue beads, not black ones or yellow or red, but blue. They were the same color as the sky on the clearest day, the same color as his eyes.

I was so surprised that I could not smile or speak. I just stood and held the four beads in my hand. I looked at them, then at him, hearing my heart beat hard.

56

He gave out presents for everyone. A shiny medal for Black Moccasin, a twist of tobacco for his son. And for the village of Metaharta, a thing that ground up corn while you stood just looking at it. Instead of pounding and pounding kernels on a stone, you put a whole corncob in a big kettle and turned a wheel round and round, and cornmeal came out the bottom. All the women cheered when they saw it.

The next day the two captains came to the lodge. They sat down at the fire and took off their moccasins, which meant that they had come as friends. Then Black Moccasin put a bearskin around each of them and they all smoked a pipe. They passed it from one to the other around the circle. Now they were friends forever.

The two men came back that night and brought some of their friends. One had a fiddle and they danced in front of the fire. They stamped their feet, kicked up their heels, and flew around in circles. Everyone enjoyed this so much that the men danced till dawn and promised to come back the next night and dance again.

This time they brought a black man with them. His name was Ben York, which was easy to say. I thought that he had painted himself black. When he was not looking I wet a finger and rubbed his arm. No black came off.

The children tried rubbing his skin, too. They pestered him until he made a face and showed his teeth and said he was a monster and would eat them alive.

He spoke no Minnetaree or Shoshone. I spoke not a word of the white man's language. But with Drewyer's help I learned that Ben York's mother and father were black, that he was born black and had been black every day since.

"This man is Captain Clark's servant," Drewyer said. "He's a slave. Where he comes from in America there are many slaves, black ones like him."

The black man saw that we were talking about him. He pushed a flock of women away and came over to where we stood. He was tall, taller than Charbonneau, and very graceful as he walked, taking long strides and swinging his arms.

"York." He pointed to himself and held up his hand with the palm out in the sign of greeting.

"Sacagawea," I said, pointing to myself.

Drewyer explained that my name meant Bird Woman. York laughed. "Do you fly like a bird?" he asked me.

"No, I fly like a bat."

"When?"

"At night when everyone sleeps," I said.

York shook his head, half believing me, and the women who had been waiting to get close rushed in and surrounded him. They still were not sure that he was really black. They did know that he was very handsome. They had never seen anyone like Ben York!

That night, when there was a big dance, the women held their breath as he jumped about and clicked his heels.

The dance lasted until the sun came up. Then Captain Lewis fired his air gun. The gun was on wheels and made of shiny brass. He pumped on the handle and suddenly it made a swishing noise and a bullet struck a tree with a loud bang.

Still, no one wanted to leave, they were so happy. Captain Clark had to call George Drewyer.

Drewyer had blue eyes and long hair streaked white by the sun. He was very tall, straight like a lodgepole, and had long, dangling arms and big hands.

He was half Shawnee and he spoke a few words in Sioux, Minnetaree, and Mandan. But he also spoke in the sign language that everyone, everywhere, in all the tribes, knew.

When Captain Clark called him out, he came forward and pointed to the eastern sky. "Menaka," he said, which is the Mandan word for sun.

Then he raised his arms and made signs and everybody took the hint and left.

Chapter Thirteen

Captain Clark changed my life. He changed everything. More than the slave hunters who came and took me from my home. More than Toussaint Charbonneau, who won me in the dreadful Hand Game. I say this before my Guardian Spirit, who may make me dead forever if I do not speak the truth.

It happened in this way. When the captains learned that Charbonneau had traded on the rivers for many years, as far to the north and west as the home of the Assiniboins and the Blackfeet and the Nez Percé, they hired him as a guide to help George Drewyer interpret Indian words for them.

They were building a camp farther along the river, where there were wide groves of cottonwood trees to use for timber. The men needed shelter against the cold. And besides this, the captains had heard that the Sioux were planning an attack sometime during the winter.

The men built a strong camp. It had two rows of huts joined together at one end, which were guarded by walls and two swivel guns. It was so strong they called it a fort, Fort Mandan—Mandan because the land belonged to the Mandan people, who were at peace with the Minnetarees.

I wanted to stay where I was, but Captain Clark made us move into the fort.

"You'll be safe here at Fort Mandan," he said. "And you can visit your Minnetaree friends anytime you wish. They're not far away."

Charbonneau told me about the pact with Captain Clark the day he was hired and we moved into the fort. He showed me the paper the captain had written on.

Even more wonderful was what Captain Clark said to Drewyer, who said to me, "The captain is hiring you just as much as your husband. He's learned that you are a Shoshone. He knows that the Shoshone live in the mountains, where he needs to travel, and that they own many fine horses, which he needs to buy. Is it true about the horses?"

"Yes," I said. "The Shoshone have many fine horses. They will wish to sell some, I think."

Captain Clark wanted to know if my father was a big man in the tribe. He also wished to know my name.

I told Drewyer my name was Sacagawea and that my father was a chieftain.

Captain Clark looked at me. "Sacagawea?" He spoke the name slowly and frowned.

He kept looking at me. He spoke to George Drewyer, who said, "He does not like the sound of Sacagawea. He wishes to call you Janey. You look like a girl he knew someplace whose name was Janey. So Janey is what he wishes to call you from this day on."

Captain Clark asked him to ask me if I liked the name.

I said "Janey" to myself. I said the name out loud. It was hard to say. It had a strange sound in my mouth.

Captain Clark was watching, waiting to see if I liked it, so I nodded my head and smiled. I did not tell him that I had another name besides Sacagawea, a secret name, which I seldom used because if you say your real name too much, it gets worn away and loses its magic.

"Janey," Captain Clark said and went on speaking fast in

60

his language. When he was done Drewyer told me what he had said.

"The captain sees that you are going to have a baby soon. He wonders if you will be able to make the long journey. To places no white man has ever seen. Over the high mountains and beyond to the big water. He wants you to go because you can help him with the horses when he comes to the land of the Shoshone. But he wonders about the baby."

I told the captain not to worry. With the baby safe on my back I would go anywhere he went, over the mountains to the big water, anywhere. The captain smiled and went away and I did not see him again until the night my son was born.

Winter came. The sun was a white ghost in the sky. It went down early and night came fast. There was no one around, except children playing, the day I fell down in pain and dragged myself to the fire and lay there and struggled for breath.

Blue Sky came. She got me into bed. I remember she put a deerskin blanket over me and a bearskin over that. I do not remember anything else until she and George Drewyer were standing beside the bed, talking to Captain Clark.

I asked where Charbonneau was. Blue Sky said he had gone to haul wood and he would be back in the morning sometime.

They went on talking, but the words sounded far away. There was a long silence. Everyone was silent, even the children. The fire was making shadows on the roof. Strange faces with gaping mouths were looking at me. Then they began to scream and I screamed back at them with all the breath I had.

I heard Blue Sky say to someone in Minnetaree, "What is to be done? She is dying."

Dying? The word soothed my pain somehow. I lay quiet. I waited for my Guardian Spirit to speak. I waited for the voices of those who were no longer living, my mother and my friends in the land of the Shoshone. I felt very calm.

Captain Clark spoke to Drewyer, who spoke to Blue Sky: "The captain has something he would like to do. He has tried it before. Sometimes it works and sometimes it does not work."

"What is it?" Blue Sky said.

"He has the rattle from a rattlesnake in his pocket and he wants to break up two of its rings. Make small pieces of them. Put them in a little water and make her swallow."

"Why not," Blue Sky said. "She is dying."

The stuff had no taste, only a scratchy feeling as it went down, but it sent me to sleep. When I woke up it was daylight and the baby was being born.

Charbonneau came soon after. He had heard the news and strode in singing. He wanted to know whether he had a son or a daughter.

"A son," I said. "We can name him Meeko."

"Meeko? What does something like that mean?"

"Little Brown Squirrel."

Charbonneau tossed his head. "No Meeko. No brown squirrel. Jean Baptiste Charbonneau," he said.

Captain Clark thought for a while. "Pompey is a fine name. Pompey Charbonneau."

Why he chose this name he did not say. It had a good sound, but not as good as Meeko, so I called my son Meeko. Not so loud that either of the men could hear it.

Drewyer said, "Captain Clark wants to know when you will be strong enough to go."

"Go now," Charbonneau said. "This girl strong Indian girl. Go now."

"A week yet. When the ice melts on the river," Captain Clark said.

He came back the next day and for five days to see how I felt. On the last day he brought Captain Lewis.

Captain Lewis had an animal with him. At first I thought it was a young buffalo. Then it came up and rubbed against me and I saw that it was a dog. But it was a dog as big as a young buffalo. It was shaggy and brown and had big gray-brown eyes. Drewyer said that its name was Scannon and that it came from a place called Newfoundland, wherever that was.

After he had rubbed against me for a while and pushed me from side to side, Scannon went over and sniffed at Meeko. The baby did not like the wet nose, but that made no difference to Scannon. He sniffed anyhow.

That day Captain Clark decided that I should learn some of the words he spoke.

That day he taught me to count from one to twenty in the white man's tongue. The next time he taught me the names of the days, and how many days made a week, and how many weeks made a month. "Night" was a new word for me. In Shoshone we always called the night a "sleep." For instance, "We traveled for six sleeps." Now I could say we traveled for six nights.

Scarcely a day went by from this time to the end of the journey that I failed to learn ten words of the white man's language. Sometimes I learned twenty words and more.

Chapter Fourteen

Meeko liked the cradleboard I made for him. He smiled the first time I put him in it. And when I took him out he screwed up his face.

This was good. Some babies in the Mandan village disliked the cradleboards. This was a big burden, because their mothers had to carry them around whatever they were doing.

With me, while I got things together for the long journey—I made an extra pair of moccasins, as well as leggings—all I had to do was to hang Meeko and his fur-lined cradleboard on a pole beside me. I never had to worry about him until it was feeding time.

When the ice broke up I was ready. But just three days before we were to leave, three traders from Canada came to the village and asked to talk to Charbonneau.

They talked for a long time. Afterward, he told me that the Canada men worked for the Northwest Company and were afraid that the Americans would ruin their trade with the Indians.

That night he woke me to say that there were many things about the journey he did not like.

"What?" I asked him. "What are they?"

"Money," he said. "Money not enough. Other things. High mountains, very high. I hear from old trader Le Blanc, long time ago. Also, many Indians. Like Assiniboins and Blackfeet. Unfriendly people, these. Slit throat, take scalp quick."

"But you gave a promise to the captains," I said.

Otter Woman was awake now. For a long time she had been telling me that it was foolish to go on such a dangerous journey among bad people and for such poor pay.

Sleepily, she said to him, "Do not listen. Go and say, 'Charbonneau wishes more money. Other things, too.'"

"I tell them," he said. "Charbonneau comes back if Charbonneau wishes. Anytime, if Toussaint Charbonneau wishes, he comes back."

"Tell them," Otter Woman said.

From the day Charbonneau was hired, the thought of going into the mountains where my people lived and seeing them again warmed my heart. The thought of the journey itself, what it was about, what Captain Clark and Captain Lewis sought, and wherever the mysterious journey led, excited me.

"You gave a promise," I said. "You cannot quit now."

He went the next morning to talk to the captains. At nightfall he returned, angry and sullen, to say that he had a fight with them.

"I tell them goodbye," he said. "No more journey. Goodbye, Captain Clark, goodbye, Captain Lewis. Goodbye."

The next day the truth came out. The captains had told him to leave and not come back. Captain Clark even said that it was me he really wanted. Not as a guide, but as someone who could help him buy horses and find his way through the country of the Shoshone.

Charbonneau brooded for a while. I begged him to go and talk to the captains again.

"Why do they want someone who quits somewhere along the trail if he feels like it?" I asked him. "If you were

Captain Clark, would you want someone like that? And if you quit, it will give you a bad name on the river."

Otter Woman kept at him, too. But she did everything she could to keep him from going. She liked her easy life traveling from one village to another, visiting places and people. But I talked, too, and at last he went back to Captain Clark and said that he was not mad anymore. He would like to go with them now.

As soon as this was over, I put everything I had made during the long winter for myself and Meeko into a deerskin bag. I put the baby and his cradleboard on my back. I said goodbye to Otter Woman, who was very pleased to be left behind.

Every day Captain Clark made black marks in a thing he called a journal. He made the marks with a stick he dipped in black paint. He said the marks were words that told everything he had seen or heard or thought that day.

When I went down to the river, he was there, sitting in one of the big boats. The journal was in his lap. He motioned me to put down the bag and the cradleboard and to sit beside him. He opened the journal, wet the stick, and put it in my hand. He put his arm around my shoulder and took my hand and guided it over the paper.

These are the things that we put in the journal together:

Fort Mandan April the 7th 1805
Sunday, at 4 o'Clock PM, the boat, in which were 6 soldiers, 2 Frenchmen and an Indian, all under the command of a corporal who had the charge of dispatches, &c.—and a canoe with 2 Frenchmen, set out down the river for St. Louis. At the same time we set out on our voyage up the river in 2 perogues and 6 canoes.

That was all I wrote while Captain Clark guided my hand. I looked at the marks as they ran back and forth on the page. I felt very proud of myself. Not until much later, when I began to learn more about the white man's language, did I know what all the marks meant.

Captain Clark wrote some more in his journal.

I saw the word "Janey," the name he had given to me. He quickly sprinkled the words with sand to dry them off. I suppose they had something to do with me.

The big silver boat that looked like a gull went down the river. Captain Lewis fired his swivel guns to say goodbye to the Mandans and we went fast up the river.

Near nightfall everyone waded to shore and I was sent out to dig roots for supper. Both of the big boats, the pirogues, were stored with food, but Captain Clark planned to use it only if nothing could be found on land. I was sent out because Charbonneau had said when the captain hired him that he should have more money because I, his wife, knew how to gather berries and all kinds of roots.

Finding roots was easy. I had done it since I was a child.

The first thing to know is where to look. The best place is around piles of driftwood. You take a sharp stick and poke until you come upon a mouse hole. Always in the hole, except at the end of winter, you will find a nest of roots from the camas bush that the mice have stored up.

The roots are as big as your thumb, white and round. They are good tasting if they are cooked with deermeat or buffalo hump.

It was the end of winter and the mice had eaten most of their store, so I had to dig long after dark. I dug enough roots for more than three dozen men.

It is best when cooking camas roots to dig a pit and put hot stones on the bottom and cover them with willow branches and lay the roots on top. You put more branches on and heap them with earth. You build a fire and let it burn until you can tell by the good smells that the roots are done.

It takes almost two days to do this. Since the men were hungry, I just boiled the roots. I dug them and cooked them because I wanted to please Captain Clark.

Charbonneau was angry. He said to Captain Clark at

supper, "Me and wife, Bird Girl, get no pay for cook. For talk. For guide. No cook."

"Janey wanted to dig the roots and cook them," Captain Clark said. "The men usually cook for themselves."

"Good," Charbonneau said. Afterward he said to me, "You no cook. Find roots, no cook. See?"

I was not displeased. To cook for three dozen hungry men was more than I could do.

We passed a Minnetaree village early the next morning, the one Le Borgne ruled over. The river runs narrow here past a low cliff and he was watching for us as we came out of the mist. He raised his hand and pointed at a huge pile of meat on the bank beside him.

"Buffalo," he shouted. "Welcome to good eating. Welcome, friends."

Captain Clark shouted back, but when Charbonneau, who was steering, turned toward shore, Captain Clark grabbed the rudder and kept us headed straight. It was well that he did. For when we floated by and left Le Borgne standing on the bank, a shower of arrows from the cliff fell upon us.

For the first time I wondered about Charbonneau. He had heard the horrible tales about Le Borgne. He knew that the one-eyed chieftain could not be trusted, that he hated the white men. Knowing this, why had Charbonneau tried to steer the boat ashore into the hands of an enemy?

Only a few days later, less than a week, I wondered even more about him. He was at the rudder of our pirogue when a gust of wind struck us and wrested the rudder from his grip. Instead of taking hold of the rudder again, he raised his hands and began to pray.

The other boats were farther up the river.

Cruzatte, the bowsman, shouted at Charbonneau, "Turn her, you fool!" Charbonneau was still praying. Cruzatte shouted again, "Turn her!"

Charbonneau was on his knees, clinging to the pirogue with one hand.

"Turn!" Cruzatte shouted again. "Turn her or I'll shoot you!"

He pointed a gun at Charbonneau's head. Charbonneau pulled hard at the rudder, but the boat stayed sideways.

The sails flapped and we tilted. Water rushed in. It swept around my knees. The baby started to cry. I saw that the shore was not far away and that I could reach it. Then I saw that our stores had begun to drift out of the boat. Charbonneau watched them drift but did not move.

Cruzatte seized the rudder.

We were floating with the current now and around us in a wide circle the water was covered with the stores that had drifted out of the boat. I saw Captain Clark's journal and a wooden box that held something he valued. He took it out of the box every day, looked at it, and carefully put it back.

Someone shouted from the shore. Waves were beating so loud against the boat I could not make out what was said, but it had a warning sound. The cradleboard had loosened. I tightened the cord that bound it to my shoulders and let myself into the water. It came up higher than my waist.

The first thing I gathered in was the wooden box. Then I grasped the journal that I had written in once and Captain Clark wrote in almost every day. A wave broke over our heads and the baby began to cry, so I gave up and climbed back in the boat.

I got safely to land but we lost most of our medicine, gunpowder, flour, melon seeds that Captain Clark was going to plant somewhere, and many other things, besides some of our beads and presents for people along the way. But I saved his journal and the wooden box. He was pleased to see them when he came back that night.

"Good as new," he said, opening the box. "I have a small one, but this is by far the best."

"What is it?" I asked him.

"A compass. You can tell whether you are traveling north or south or east or west. Otherwise you get lost."

He was so pleased that he kissed me on the cheek and gave me a beautiful gift. It was an antelope belt sewn with rows of tiny blue beads. It was so beautiful my throat choked up and I couldn't thank him.

After supper I asked Charbonneau why he had not obeyed Cruzatte.

"Hear nothing," he said. "Hear wind, hear water. No hear Cruzatte."

A tight look around his mouth made me think he was telling a lie. He had heard Cruzatte.

"You think something?" he asked me, clenching his hands. "You think Charbonneau hear, huh?"

I shook my head.

I began to wonder. I remembered the day the traders had talked to him. How that night he had told me that they were afraid the Americans would ruin their business. How the next day he had told Captain Clark he would not go with him. And how, the very next day, he had changed his mind and decided to go.

Was it possible that he had some secret with the Canada traders? Had they hired him to make trouble?

"You think things?" he asked, still clenching his hands.

"Nothing," I said.

"You jump in river. Near drown. Jean Baptiste near drown. Jean Baptiste Charbonneau worth more than captains. More than Bird Girl. Anybody. See?"

"Yes," I said.

If his son meant that much to him, why had he tried to destroy the boat and take the chance that Meeko might drown? Why had he sat with his hands in the air and prayed, deaf to Cruzatte's commands? I did not dare to ask him.

"What you think?" he said. "You think Charbonneau hear Cruzatte, huh?"

"No."

"Good," he said and unclenched his fists. "Good."

70

Chapter Fifteen

Besides the other things, we lost all of our flour and most of the pemmican. It was a bad loss. Captain Clark said that now we had to live on the roots we gathered and the animals our hunters shot.

We saw no animals the next few days, except the many buffalo that had died in the ice during the winter and a bear that ran from our hunters. To the west where the prairie stretched farther than the eye could see, the banks were covered with flowering bushes. But it was much too early for berries. So I dug roots every night when we stopped and they were cooked with the last of the pemmican.

The river was shallow. Yet currents ran strong. Wading in mud up to their knees, stumbling over rocks and logs, the men pulled on ropes fastened to the bow of each boat. Men on the boats had long poles that they thrust into the water at the bow and stern.

If the wind blew right, sails were raised on the pirogues. But mostly the men clawed their way up the river. Those with the small canoes had less trouble, yet everyone suffered. Boiled camas root with a few shreds of pemmican was not enough for men who toiled so hard from dawn to nightfall.

Captain Lewis asked everyone to look for animals—antelope, bears, deer, or buffalo. He sent bands of hunters out to search both sides of the river.

Soon after the bad accident, a grizzly bear was sighted. It was shambling along the shore of a sandbar in the middle of the river, a sandbar like the one I had lived on when I fled from Le Borgne.

Bearmeat is not the best meat to be found, being tough to the teeth and musky on the tongue. Besides, bears are dangerous. But Captain Lewis had no choice. He sent Captain Clark out to bring back bearmeat.

Captain Clark, Sergeant Ordway, and a hunter got ready. As they were about to set off the grizzly came out of the bush with a cub.

"It is black luck to kill a bear that has a young one at her side," I said to Captain Clark.

He looked at me as if he thought there might be nothing in my head.

"It is black luck," I said.

"My men are hungry. What would you have us do, starve?"

"There are other bears, without young, to kill," I said.

"Where? We have traveled for nine days. This is the first we've had a chance to kill."

Charbonneau was in the water, pulling the boat ashore. He stopped and gave me a disgusted look. "Crazy talk," he said. "Crazy Shoshone talk."

The bear had seen us and had gone into the heavy brush in the center of the sandbar. She took the cub with her.

Captain Lewis called to Captain Clark, "Take your hunters and follow them." To Charbonneau he said, "Get back in the boat and stay. Watch what happens. Be ready to pull away should you need to!"

Two hunters waded to the sandbar and took up their places. With his rifle on his shoulder, Captain Clark stood not far from me on the shore.

The hunter at the far end of the sandbar fired into the brush. The bear came out, swaying her head from side to side. She glanced along the bank, first at the hunter whose gun was still smoking, then at Sergeant Ordway, then at Captain Clark.

I was wearing the belt of blue beads that Captain Clark had given me. It caught the sun. The bear's eyes fastened upon me. She was making up her mind which one of us to attack.

"Crazy bear," Charbonneau said, getting ready to put the boat back into the river. "Like crazy womans. What she do, no telling. Crazy."

I turned away so he would not see me. I closed my eyes and prayed. I asked the Great Spirit to spare the mother and her cub. I prayed that she would flee back into the brush. Night was coming on. If they did not kill her now, she would be safe. I prayed until I heard a second shot.

Captain Clark had fired his gun. He was wrapped in a cloud of yellow smoke. Dust spurted up from the bear's furry hide. She fell to her knees, but quickly she gathered herself and rose to her full height. She was taller than a tall man.

Someone shot and missed. The bear did not move. She was watching Captain Clark. He was the closest to her of the hunters, not ten short strides away. I saw the danger he was in. I must have uttered a warning, for Charbonneau became angry.

"Clark no child of Sacagawea," he said. "Clark no husband of Sacagawea. Why Sacagawea make big fuss?"

I did not answer him. This was the first time that I knew how I truly felt about Captain Clark. My heart beat so hard I could not have spoken if I wanted to.

The bear no longer stood on her hind legs. She was watching Captain Clark. He took out a paper tube with gunpowder in it and a ball. He tore the tube open with his teeth and poured powder into the pan. He crumpled the brown paper around the ball and put it into the barrel.

The bear sniffed the air. I think she smelled the bitter smell of the powder.

She moved toward him. She lifted her paws high at each step she took. It might have been the sounds the river made, but I was sure that I heard her claws crunch into the sand. There was blood running down her shoulder. She paused to lick it off.

The hunters fired twice and the bear fell. But while the hunters began to load their guns again, while Captain Clark finished loading his, the bear was on her feet once more. She staggered toward him. She growled with rage and her eyes were a fiery red.

The hunters shouted. "Run," I screamed as loud as I could.

I jumped out of the boat and waded into the river. The baby in his cradleboard was on my back. Captain Clark was in the river. He braced himself against the current and fired his gun. One of the hunters also fired.

When she was dragged out of the water and laid on the bank, the men found five bullets. One was sunk deep in her heart. The men said that her flesh was dry and stringy, yet they ate all of it that night. They were making up for the days without meat.

In the morning we left early. The cub stood at the edge of the brush, but Captain Lewis was in too much of a hurry to take time to hunt it down.

We saw more and more grizzly bears as we moved north. One of the men was chased by a bear and saved himself only by climbing a tree. Captain Lewis stumbled upon a white bear one noon and saved himself by leaping from a very high bank into the river. Bears sniffed around our camp at night, two or three at a time, and would have attacked us had it not been for Scannon. He had a keen nose for bears, a mean growl, and a loud bark.

But Scannon knew nothing about beavers. One morning we came to a place where some huge cottonwoods were piled up. Beavers had cut them down and were at work making a dam.

Scannon was beside me in the canoe. He saw the animals swimming around, their coats shining in the sun. One was chewing on a tree. Beaver teeth are long and wide and curved like a chisel. While you watch they can gnaw through a tree trunk with a few quick bites.

I have no idea what he thought about these glossy things with the tails that looked like paddles. He might have thought they were big squirrels. Anyway, he jumped out of the canoe and grabbed the first one he came to.

Then, just as he seized the beaver by the tail, it turned and caught the tip of his nose. He shook his head and growled. The animal held on. I yelled at him and he swam back to me. But the beaver did not let go until Charbonneau killed it with a blow of his fist.

Scannon hurt for days. He lay in the canoe too sick to raise his head. Captain Clark treated his jaws with medicine and I made him eat. Everyone thought that he would die. But he was a strong dog and lived. He was smart, too. He never went near a beaver again.

During the time Scannon was sick, we had to guard against the bears. Men walked around the camp all night with rifles and watched.

They watched for bears more than they watched for Sioux or Blackfeet. That is why we had a bad surprise one day during the time Scannon was sick.

It was near dusk and we had made an early camp because the day had been hard on the men. Most of them were on the shore, pulling the boats, struggling through heavy growths of prickly pear. The thorns had cut their hands and pierced their moccasins. Captain Clark himself had two thorns in his back and seventeen thorns, half as long as my finger, were stuck in his feet.

The men were sitting by the fire, too tired to talk or even eat. We were camped in a cottonwood grove. Leaves stirred in the wind and the river was making sounds along the bank.

Warriors who looked like Assiniboins came out of the trees. They came silently but if Scannon had been well he would have heard them. It was a large band, twice our number. They carried bows and sacks of arrows. They stood in a row between us and the river, so we could not reach our boats, our cannon, or the firesticks.

A young man with a roach, hair cut short on two sides of his skull and the hair in the middle painted green, said that he was Chief Green Cat. He wanted to know who we were, why we were there, and where we were going.

Drewyer answered his questions. He stood up and pointed to Captain Clark and Captain Lewis.

Chief Green Cat's warriors had their hair cut like his and their chests were painted with stripes and swirls. Green circles around their eyes made them look like prowling wolves.

Their chieftain shook his head and spoke to Drewyer. Drewyer said that the chieftain thought we had come to make trouble. Big trouble.

There were two guns lying beside the fire. Green Cat put a foot on them. His warriors quietly strung their bows.

Captain Clark got to his feet. He told us to be calm and not to move. "We don't stand much of a chance in a fight. We'll lose men and maybe our canoes."

I was sitting with my back against a tree, away from the fire, nursing my baby.

"Green Cat hasn't seen you yet," Captain Clark said to me. "Come here by the fire."

I put Meeko in the cradleboard and went and stood beside him. Green Cat looked at me. He saw the cradleboard. He heard Meeko fuss and cry, now that the nursing had ended.

For a while Chief Green Cat was silent. He glanced at his feet, then at me. Then, without a word, he picked up the two guns lying in the grass. Then he motioned to his warriors and they went back into the cottonwood trees as silently as they had come.

The men felt better. They forgot that they were tired. They remembered that they had not eaten since dawn. I got my pointed stick and started off to look for camas roots.

Captain Clark stopped me. He put an arm around my shoulder.

"You're much better than Scannon," he said. "Scannon would bark at the first sound. We'd reach for our muskets. People would be killed. As it is, we're all alive, with the loss of only two guns."

He took the digging stick, gave me a hug, and went off to dig camas roots.

Soon afterward, when Scannon was over his beaver bite, we had another bad time. Almost as bad as the one with the Assiniboins. It happened this way.

Soon after supper, while the camp was asleep, our sentinel was startled by loud barks from Scannon. The sentinel, Sergeant Pryor, told us what happened then.

A big moon was shining on the water. The sentinel thought the dog was barking at it. But after a time he heard something splashing around and saw a bull buffalo swimming across the river.

The bull got ashore, clambered over our boats, and climbed the bank. He was huge, Sergeant Pryor said.

The beast stopped on the bank and looked around, then started for our tents. He charged through the fires, kicking up a shower of sparks. He was close to our tents, right on them, the sergeant said, when Scannon rushed at him. The bull changed his course and went crashing through the trees.

We were all awake by this time, me with the baby in my arms, the men with the guns, staring at one another, asking the sentinel what had happened.

Scannon was a hero soon again. A bull elk was grazing along the bank in front of us. As we came nearer, George

Drewyer, our best hunter, wounded it with a single shot and the elk started to run away.

Scannon had been catching squirrels most of the day, bringing them back for Captain Lewis, who liked them better than any other meat. The dog was worn down, breathing hard with his huge mouth open and his tongue hanging out. But he roused himself and jumped out of the canoe. He overtook the elk, wrestled it into the river, and hung on until the beast drowned.

Captain Lewis gave him an elk bone to gnaw, a big one. Scannon begged for more.

The men welcomed the good elk meat. They had worn thin. For a long time now no two days were alike. Half-naked and burned brown as Blackfeet, they struggled with the balky canoes. One day they tramped in deep mud along the shore, pulling on the ropes. The next day the shore might be thick with prickly pears or slippery with loose rocks. Often they pushed the boats with poles. When the river was shallow they waded in and pushed. Sometimes they had to climb along a steep bluff holding the towlines. There were very few days with enough wind to use the sails. I looked at the men and wondered why they did not give up.

The day after Scannon's feat our hunters killed two more elk, but it was a hard day like all the rest. And late in the afternoon a cloud of clacking black-spotted grasshoppers descended upon us. A hot wind blew them against us so hard that I had to cover Meeko with a blanket and lie down in the bottom of the canoe.

It was a bad day—we made only seven miles up the river—but that night Cruzatte got out his fiddle, Sergeant Ordway got out the tambourine, and Drewyer got out the sounding horn. We built a big fire and banked elk ribs against it. The men sat around the fire and cut slices of the fat meat for themselves, told stories, and sang songs of home.

Chapter Sixteen

How the sickness came upon me was a mystery. Early the next day, before dawn, I woke sweating all over. By sunrise I was cold, as if my bood had turned to water. I was too sick to make a fire, which I did every morning. Charbonneau came and stood over me.

"Why you sleep?" he wanted to know. "Charbonneau hungry. Captain Clark, he hungry. What for no fire?"

I was too weak to answer. Even when he gave me a prod with his foot, I said nothing.

Captain Clark got up and looked at me. He put his hand on my forehead. "The girl is feverish," he said to Charbonneau. "You make the fire while I give her some medicine."

The medicine, a spoonful of black stuff in a cup of water, felt bitter in my throat. Worse, much worse, then the pieces of snake rattle they made me swallow the day Meeko was born.

It did no good. When they were ready to leave I was so weak they had to carry me to the boat.

I lay all that morning with a heavy blanket over me, though the sun was hot. I watched the sun move among the clouds, casting light, then shadows. In the shadows I saw strange faces I had never seen before. I shut my eyes in fear of them until the sun came out again.

Captain Clark gave me another cup of the black stuff. Twice I roused myself to nurse the baby, but that was all.

The river ran swift that day. The men with the poles pushing and those near the bank pulling on the ropes tired early. Captain Clark decided to make camp long before nightfall. He was worried about my sickness. I heard him outside the tent talking to Captain Lewis and Charbonneau. I understood most of what was said.

"What if she dies?" Captain Lewis said. "What can we do with the baby? We can't drag it across the mountains, all the way to the sea. It can't eat buffalo or deermeat or duck or goose. It drinks milk. We have no milk. I say send her back to Fort Mandan before something happens. There'll be some woman at the fort who can feed the baby."

"It's better to take a chance on her getting well," Captain Clark said. "For one thing, the men all like her. She livens their spirits. And just as important, she has a good effect upon the Indians we meet. Seeing a girl and a baby with us, they see that we mean them no harm and wish to be friends. Another thing: we are coming into mountain country that she knows, where we'll no longer need boats but the horses she can find for us. We need this girl badly."

"What do you say?" Captain Lewis asked Charbonneau. "You are her husband."

I was not surprised at his answer.

"She die, Jean Baptiste Charbonneau die," he said. "Better we go back. Quick!"

I was not surprised, because I knew why he wanted to return to Fort Mandan. He had not wanted to leave in the first place. He had fought with the captains and only made up with them when I argued him into it. I still wondered about the Canada men. Did he have a secret pact with them?

"Wait until morning," Captain Clark said. "I'll bleed her tonight. Take a pint of blood."

"No more," Captain Lewis said.

"I wish we had leeches, but I've seen none on the Missouri, except in human form."

"There's only one sharp knife left out of the three we owned before the boat turned over."

"One's enough," Captain Clark said. "If it's sharp."

Whether the knife was sharp I do not know. They gave me another cup of the black stuff and I felt nothing when they drained my blood.

But in the morning I felt weaker than I ever had and fell into a long dream. I woke up with the sun in my eyes. Later I found out that two days and nights had gone by. The boat was moving along under a bower of trees.

For a while I thought Charbonneau and I were alone with Meeko and we were going back down the river, back to Fort Mandan, the three of us.

Then Captain Clark was looking at me. "You're better," he said. "You'll live. You look like a ghost, but a pretty ghost, and you will live."

"Where are we?" I asked him. I still believed that I was in a canoe with Charbonneau and my baby, going back down the river.

"We're in Blackfoot country. At least they claim it. Do you know any of their words?"

"Not many. A word or two, maybe. They raided the Shoshone long ago when I was a child. They are fierce people."

"They don't like the whites."

"They do not like anyone, only themselves," I said. "And not always themselves."

"You would know Blackfeet if you saw them from a distance? Their dress, their horses?"

"Yes, I would know them anywhere, also their footprints. They do not walk with their toes pointed in like the Minnetarees or the Shoshone."

"We saw a campfire yesterday and some tracks. Charbonneau thought they belonged to a party of Sioux."

"This is too far north and west for the Sioux. They do not come here in the spring. I learned this from the Minnetarees."

Two days later I had a chance to show my knowledge of the Blackfeet. One of the men who was pulling a long rope fished a headband with an eagle feather tied to it out of the river. The feather looked like any eagle feather, but the band I knew at once. It was red, a color the Blackfeet liked. The sewing, the way the sun was stitched, with arrows sticking out from it, was Blackfoot. Once my brother killed a Blackfoot and kept his headband. It was just like the headband they fished out of the river.

That night Captain Lewis mounted a bigger guard than he usually did and all the men slept in their clothes. We mounted a guard for seven nights and during the day watched for signs. We watched for buffalo too.

On the eighth day Ben York saw a small cloud off to the west. We were on a wide bend below a high cliff. Captain Clark ordered the boats to tie up on the riverbank.

He chose four hunters and Charbonneau, York, and me. Me because he believed that the Blackfeet would not attack us if they saw a woman. Charbonneau because he was my husband and very jealous. Ben York because he had sharp eyes and ears and a keen nose. He could smell buffalo when they were a long distance away. Buffalo had a strong smell, but he could smell them before anyone else did.

The high cliff above the river was where Captain Clark was taking us. "To look over the country," he said.

Since he was worried about the Blackfeet, I thought it best to leave Meeko behind. I had never left him since the day he was born. He was always nearby in the cradleboard, whatever I was doing. So I asked the men who played with him the most, Sergeant Ordway and Private Cruzatte, to take care of him while I was gone.

It was a hard climb through brush and prickly pear. We came out on a windy peak. Below us was a broad tableland. I could see nothing except the cloud of blue smoke, but Ben York threw his head back and sniffed the wind for a while. Then he pointed.

"Look," he shouted. "There to the west, beyond the smoke. A speck. It's buffalo!"

The speck grew larger. It became a river, a dark river of buffalo, driven along the tableland by a string of horsemen.

"Who are they?" Captain Clark asked Charbonneau. "Blackfeet?"

"No," Charbonneau said. "Arikara, maybe. Assiniboin, maybe."

The captain asked me who the horsemen were. I knew, but I was silent. I did not want to go against my husband. Not until the captain asked me a second time did I answer.

"It's important," he said. "We don't want to run into a nest of Blackfeet if we can help it. Who are they, Janey?"

"Blackfeet, I think."

"You think they are Blackfeet or you know?"

"I know."

Charbonneau grunted. "You wrong, you Shoshone. Maybe Arikara. Maybe Assiniboin."

I spoke up now because it was important. "Blackfeet," I said.

"How do you know?" Captain Clark said.

"Because Blackfeet ride black horses that have white spots on their backs."

The herd came closer. Not to be seen, we crouched in the bushes. A man on foot was running ahead of the herd. He was dressed in a buffalo robe and wore a buffalo head that came down over his shoulders. He looked like a buffalo.

The man lured the herd on and on, into a draw, close to the edge of a cliff. He dodged behind a tree. The leaders could not turn back, for the rest of the great herd pressed hard behind them. The big part of the herd could not turn

83

back because the horsemen were on their heels, shouting and firing their guns.

Like a river the buffalo poured over the cliff, down like falling water to their deaths on the plain below.

We waited three days for the Blackfeet to cut up the buffalo and leave. They took only a small part of what they had killed. Hundreds of carcasses were left. Of these we took only what we could store in the boats.

The young hunter who lured the herd over the cliff had been swept out of his hiding place to his death. The Blackfeet had wrapped him in a buffalo hide and tied him high in a tree, as was their custom, to keep him safe from hungry beasts.

"That's how I would like to be buried," Ben York said. "In a tree where the wind blows, the sun shines, and the birds sing."

"Yes," I said, "but not soon."

"Years from now would be best."

Captain Clark was walking around gathering flowers from the bushes.

"He has gathered things every day since we left Fort Mandan," I said. "Why?"

"He gathers them for the Great Grand White Chief, Thomas Jefferson," York said. "But Captain Lewis gathers much more."

"This White Chief is like Chief Black Moccasin?"

"Like a buffalo is like a mosquito."

"If he is so great, why does he want such things as skunk skins, small fish, goat horns, hummingbird feathers, antelope skins, deerskin, buffalo hides, beaver tails, and other things, too, like owls, snakes, frogs, and lizards?"

"Thomas Jefferson has a big curiosity. That's why we are here, you and all of us."

Captain Clark had quit gathering flowers. "How far have you been up the river?" he asked Charbonneau.

Charbonneau pointed to the snow-covered mountains. "Far, to Blackfoot country."

This was a lie. Just the day before he had told me that everything was new. He had never been in this country before.

"River, she too thin," he said. "Need horses."

Captain Clark was impatient. "Where do we find the horses?"

"From Mandans."

"We turn around and go back to Fort Mandan?"

"Good," Charbonneau said. He did not see that Captain Clark was angry. "Hide canoes. Go back. Go talk to Mandans. Get horses."

Captain Clark shook his head. "If we do, we'll never reach the mountains before winter comes. There's snow on them now and this is June. By November we'll be caught and can't move."

He picked up his flowers and left with Sergeant Ordway. Charbonneau waited until they were out of hearing. "Tonight," he said. "We go down river. Fast!"

He reached out and gave my arm a twist to remind me about what would happen if I did not hold my tongue.

"You think Captain Clark great mans," he said. "You crazy Shoshone. Shoshone they all crazy. Gone now. Blackfeet came and kill them. Your family gone now—dead."

This was a lie also. He was making up the story because he knew that I had never forgotten my people. I never talked about them, but he knew that one reason I wanted to go on the long journey was to see them again, the ones who were still alive.

"Blackfeet kill Jean Baptiste. My son, Jean Baptiste Charbonneau. Kill him, sure."

Were the Blackfeet just an excuse? Or was he sure that Clark would fail? Sure that we would never reach the mountains before the heavy snows came?

That night in the tent, when Sergeant Ordway and Captain Clark were asleep, Charbonneau took the baby and went down to the river. He knew that I would follow him. I put on my moccasins quietly, but as I left the tent I stepped hard on Sergeant Ordway's outstretched hand. He got up, rubbed his eyes, and uttered a loud oath.

"Come!" I whispered.

Charbonneau knelt in the canoe. The cradleboard was beside him. I put Meeko and the cradleboard on my back. A fire burned in front of the tent. Suddenly from the dark, a rifle spurted flame.

Crouched, holding a paddle in his hands, Charbonneau shouted at me. Sergeant Ordway was standing on the bank. He fired his rifle again. As the bullet struck the water in front of the canoe, Charbonneau dropped the paddle.

"Go to sleep," Sergeant Ordway said. "More prickly pears tomorrow, more mud, more slippery stones, more everything. Go to sleep, we'll need you."

Charbonneau grunted. "Much everything."

Chapter Seventeen

Before we started the next morning, Captain Clark came to the tent where Charbonneau was stretched out in front of the fire, eating his breakfast.

Captain Clark was wrapped in a buffalo robe against the cold. His eyes looked angry. "What happened last night?" he asked. "Sergeant Ordway tells me that he found you in one of the canoes, about to bid us farewell. Is that true?"

Charbonneau had a quick answer. "Shoshone here, she wake Charbonneau. She cry many tears. She beg take her back to Minnetaree. She fraid of Blackfeet. Fraid for baby, Jean Baptiste Charbonneau."

Captain Clark waited for me to say something. I put Meeko in his cradleboard and said nothing. I had learned, I had been warned to hold my tongue.

"My wife, she Shoshone. Afraid everything," Charbonneau said. "We leave now. Sorry, too bad."

"You can leave if you want to. I'll pay you the money we owe," Captain Clark said. "But you can't take a canoe. We need every one we have."

Charbonneau grumbled. "Me walk, huh?"

"You walk," Captain Clark said.

"Long way."

"Yes, a very long way."

Captain Clark turned his back on us and went down to the river.

Charbonneau ate the last piece of his boiled buffalo. He picked it up, held it in his jaws, and cut it in two with his knife. Then he wiped his mouth on his beard and went to fold our tent. As soon as he was gone I followed Captain Clark. He was putting the things he had gathered the day before in his canoe.

"I don't want to see you go," he said. "The men will miss you. You've kept up their spirits. They tell themselves, 'If a girl with a baby on her back can do this day after day, then we can too.' They keep going when they would like to quit."

"Charbonneau did not speak for me," I said. "He lied when he told you that I woke him in the night and wept and begged him to take me back to Fort Mandan. It was a lie, Captain Clark. I did not weep and I did not beg."

"Do you want to go with us?" he said.

"Yes."

"But you're afraid of what Charbonneau will say?"

"No, of what he will do. He has a bad temper."

"We need you," he said. "The journey has been hard so far, but from here on into the high mountains it will be worse. Dangerous. Do you understand what I am telling you?"

"I understand."

"Still you want to go?"

"I do."

"I'll not hold it against you if you turn back. You'll be safe. The baby will be safe. You're sure you want to go?"

There was nothing, nothing that would make me turn back. Wherever he led, I would go.

"Yes," I said. "I am sure."

Dawn was breaking. The sun shone through the trees. It

turned his hair to bright copper. He looked like the God of the Gods Above.

Charbonneau sidled up to the pirogue and tossed his blankets over the rail. He got into a canoe and took up a paddle. Cruzatte, Drewyer, and Captain Lewis were in the canoe. He spoke to them in a friendly voice as though nothing had happened. He even smiled at me. He asked me when I was going to feed Jean Baptiste Charbonneau again.

"Now in buffalo country," he said. "Soon Charbonneau kill buffalo. Good food, this buffalo. Buffalo hump best. Cook big hump for Jean Baptiste."

I told him that the baby had no teeth to chew with.

"When does teeth come?" he asked.

"Not tomorrow."

"Jean Baptiste, he different. Son of Charbonneau many teeth soon. Chew buffalo like Charbonneau hisself."

We saw thousands of buffalo the next day. They grazed in herds, on and on, to the horizon. Packs of gray wolves trotted beside them, circling the herds like trusty watchmen. They were waiting for an animal to get injured or a calf to stray, so they could pounce on it.

Charbonneau and the hunters went out and came back with meat from seven buffalo, enough to last us for a week. As he promised, Charbonneau brought a hump for Meeko and also three lengths of treepies, which are milky-white intestines. He had me stuff them with the chopped hump meat. Then he tried to feed a piece to Meeko, who did not like treepies any more than I did. So Charbonneau had to settle for feeding him spoonfuls of broth.

We saw buffalo every day for another week and the hunters brought back all the meat they could carry, which I smoked and made pemmican of. We saw two Blackfoot camps. In one of them I found a woman's tracks. They had a strange look to me until I remembered that Blackfeet cut off the toes of all their women who are loose with themselves.

That night Captain Lewis ordered us to sleep in our

89

moccasins and we kept a big fire going. The Blackfeet were good at crawling up to a tent without being seen.

They were brutal, these Blackfeet. There were three tribes of them—the Bloods and the Piegans and the Blackfeet themselves, who gave their name to the other two. They were the first to feel insulted about something. The first to break their word. The first to steal and burn and murder.

We watched for them the next day as we went up the river toward the snowy peaks far away against the sky. We saw no signs, but there was still another problem for Captain Lewis and Captain Clark. It was even more important than the hostile Blackfeet.

At noon that day we came to a wide river, not as wide as the river we were following, but swift and troubled. The river we were on the Minnetarees called Amahte Arzzha. The captains called it the Missouri. The Minnetarees had made a map for us showing the troubled river, which they called the River That Scolds at All the Others. Captain Lewis thought of a girl he had known for some time and named it Maria's River.

Before we left, a deep hole was dug in the middle of an island and everything heavy that we could do without was buried, also some provisions, tools, and powder and lead. The red pirogue was hauled out, tied to a tree, and covered with brush so the Blackfeet would not find it.

It rained all night, hard. But in the morning, the land stretched away like a great silver lake. The far mountains glittered. The magpies flashed their black and white feathers. I picked a flower for Meeko to smell. Instead, he opened his rosebud mouth and tried to eat it.

We were at the branching of two large rivers. Which one would lead us to the mountains before the fierce winter storms shut them away? The captains talked for a day but could not decide. Charbonneau said that Maria's River was the best to take, which made Captain Clark believe that the Missouri was the best.

The captains talked for another day. Then they went off in different directions, climbed hills, and looked through spyglasses. When they came back, they decided to take the south fork, Amahte Arzzha, the Missouri.

Charbonneau and I were in our canoe, getting ready to leave the River That Scolds at All the Others. Both the captains were walking along the shore, still not sure that we should follow the Missouri. York was in the canoe just in front of us. A breeze had come up and he was raising a sail to catch it.

"What do you think?" he called back to Charbonneau. "The Missouri winds like a snake. Seems to me it winds too much."

"Both wind too much," Charbonneau called to York. "Make head dizzy, huh, black man?"

Our sail caught the breeze, but York's canoe was moving away from us. Charbonneau dug his paddle deep, his huge shoulders heaved, and we came up close to York.

For three days now, since the day the current grew strong, York was sent ashore to pull on one of the ropes. Most days he was in Captain Lewis's canoe, helping the captain as a servant, handing him a spyglass or whatever he asked for. The banks where he had to walk were thick with thorns. His feet were so swollen he could barely move around.

"You sick man," Charbonneau called to him. "Maybe you die quick. Better go home."

York did not answer.

"Crazy black man," Charbonneau grumbled. "He slave man. All time do what captain say. Like big slave, like Shoshone."

Quietly I said, "Before you married me, then I was a slave. Now I am not a slave."

"Not now, not now. But soon you slave. Soon, like crazy black man. Like Indians, too. Indians everyplace slaves soon."

"We gave our word to go with the captains, remember? To help them."

"Charbonneau, he say no. Shoshone say yes. Shoshone say go. Not Toussaint Charbonneau, remember, huh?"

The cradleboard was turned toward him. He must have reached out and touched Meeko, for my son gave his shy little laugh.

"Jean Baptiste, he no slave," Charbonneau said. "Jean Baptiste Charbonneau, he no slave, see?"

A shadow, Charbonneau's broad paddle, hung above my head. "Yes, I see."

We went for a day through heavy rain, but the land was beautiful and covered with buffalo. Captain Clark said there must be more than ten thousand of them feeding on the deep grass.

Our men were suffering again from the prickly pears they had to walk through. Their moccasins were so pierced with thorns that they were nearly barefoot. Captain Clark sent hunters out to gather hides to make new ones.

Some of the buffalo were grazing along the riverbank. They stopped to look at the canoes but did not flee. Hunters in the first canoe fired and killed one of them. A third and fourth shot struck an enormous bull. He started to run away, but after a fifth shot broke one of his back legs, he turned to face us.

The bull hobbled as far as the riverbank and stopped. He braced himself and rolled his head from side to side, searching for the enemy. Blood streamed from his mouth. Beneath the matted forelock, his eyes were closing with death, but he braced himself and bellowed. His body swayed. He fell to his knees. A moaning gasp came from his throat and he rolled over on his side and lay still.

Charbonneau said, "Sometime no buffalo. White men kill them. No buffalo anywhere."

I scraped two of the hides from the ten buffalo the hunters killed, fed the fire that smoked them, and helped to make moccasins for some of the men. My husband did not need a pair because he had refused from the start to wade over slippery rocks or struggle along the bank through stands of thorn bushes, pulling on a rope.

Hunters killed more buffalo. Baskets of fat trout were caught and smoked. We got ready to go up the Missouri toward the Great Falls the Minnetarees and Mandans had told us about. Toward the Shining Mountains we could see against the sky. Shining because they were always covered with snow.

Before we left, Captain Lewis had a wonderful day. In a red willow thicket he found a young owl sitting in a nest. It was white and no larger than his fist. He had never seen one like it before. He sat down and held it in his lap while he wrote in his journal. He put down how many claws the owl had and how many wing feathers, the color of its eyes, on and on. He was so excited he let his breakfast get cold.

Chapter Eighteen

We were ready to leave, but then Captain Lewis had a problem. He still was not sure which river to follow, the River That Scolds at All the Others or the Amahte Arzzha, the Missouri River.

He decided to take some men and go up the south fork and look for the Great Falls. If he found them, it meant that the south fork was the river that led to the Shining Mountains.

He was gone for two weeks nearly. The men's clothes were falling apart, so they spent the evenings while he was gone making jackets and trousers for themselves. I worked hard to help them—too hard, I guess, for I fell sick. I could not raise my head. I managed to nurse my son and that was all I could do. Poor baby with a sick mother. What a wonder that he ever lived!

Captain Clark made a cut on my arm with the knife that he kept in his pocket and bled me three times and fed me some strong medicine. By the time Captain Lewis got back, I felt better, though I could do nothing but sit in the sun.

Captain Clark saw that I had the best food, like marrow bones, boiled buffalo hump, and suet dumplings. When

Captain Lewis came back and told him all that he saw when he reached the Great Falls, Captain Clark sat down by the fire and repeated the story to me.

"Captain Lewis was going along on a level plain when suddenly he heard the sound of falling water. He moved farther toward the sound and saw spray rising from the plain like a pillar of smoke. At once he knew that he was approaching the Great Falls of the Missouri.

"Then Captain Lewis climbed to a high rock near the center of the falls. Below him was a cliff and over it the water was falling in a great fury. The flowing water took on a thousand shapes. It flew up in streamers many times the height of his head. Beneath them the water rolled and swelled in huge billows that struck against the rocks and shook the earth."

I went to sleep listening to his story about the Great Falls. In the morning I rose with the sun and felt strong enough to build a fire and cook breakfast for Charbonneau and myself.

Charbonneau said, "Captain Clark, he worry. Afraid you die. Afraid he get no horses from Shoshone if you dead. So Charbonneau, he ask for money, I think?"

He did ask Captain Clark for more money. He said that without me they would never find the horses they needed to get through the mountains before the snows came. Captain Clark refused him. For days while we were making ready to leave, Charbonneau went around in silence and would not lend a hand at anything.

Captain Lewis had brought word that there were five big falls on the river he had traveled, so it was necessary now to travel with carts and on foot. Six men were chosen to make carts with wheels, bodies, and fastenings out of a cotton-wood tree.

Captain Lewis had a special canoe. The frame was made of iron covered with deerhide. It was twelve strides long. He said it would be easier to carry now that we had to leave the river and travel by land. He had saved it for just this

95

time. But when he put it in the water the canoe sank, and he lost his best compass and other valuable things. Two new dugouts had to be made to take its place.

Captain Clark went out to look at the way we had to travel to get around the falls. He came back with word that it was over level land but eighteen miles long and covered thickly with prickly pears. He marked the way we were to travel with stakes and little flags.

The men hid the big pirogue on White Bear Island, which was near our camp. (They hid it there because the island was infested with bears. Thieving Blackfeet would be afraid to go to such a wild place.) The dugouts were carried up the bluff and put on the two carts, and we started off on the portage that was to last for more than eighteen very bad miles.

Those miles were bad because of the many things that happened to us. On the first day it hailed. The next day it snowed. Then the sun came out, scorching hot. Overnight, a violent wind blew and black clouds rose in the west.

Captain Clark, Charbonneau, Ben York, and I—with Meeko in my arms, not in his cradleboard, because something had frightened him and he was crying—were in a deep gully not far from the river.

Charbonneau said, "The sky, she ugly up there. Better we get under trees."

"Better yet," Captain Clark said, "we'll look for a cave."

But there were no trees or caves. We were in a gully strewn with cactus.

Captain Clark led us along the riverbank to the head of the ravine. Here he found a rocky shelf that would give us some shelter from the rain and from the wind that had blown violently on the first day of the portage. If the wind blew again, we were now so near the bank that without this shelter we might easily be swept into the river.

Charbonneau and Captain Clark put down their guns.

Captain Clark took off his jacket and laid it over his compass and a parcel of berries he had found on the way. Ben York climbed out of the ravine and went off to hunt buffalo.

Lightning flashed. Thunder echoed. The ravine was filled with a yellow light and thunderous sounds.

The rain fell gently at first, mixed with large hailstones. Suddenly it fell in a glittering mass that hid the sky.

Through the rain and hail I saw a yellow wall gathering at the head of the ravine. It was moving toward us. Before I could find the cradleboard, before I could shout a warning, Captain Clark had me by the arm. He was pushing me and the baby up a steep cliff.

Charbonneau had clambered ahead already. He reached down and caught the sleeve of my jacket, but he was so terrified that he could not hold on.

"Save yourself!" I shouted to him. "We are safe."

But we were not safe. With one hand I desperately clung to the baby. With the other I grasped a bush that grew in a crack between two rocks.

The rock I stood upon was slippery and narrow but it slanted away from the cliff. I could see nothing above me. When I looked up, hailstones stung my face.

I glanced down at Captain Clark, who was clinging to a rock below me. His hat, which had a cord that came under his chin and held it on his head, was gone. His hair was in his eyes. He brushed it away and tried to smile.

Below us the yellow flood roared through the gully. It pushed rocks and brush before it and surged over the precipice. It was deep, higher than my head. Meeko's cradleboard, Captain Clark's compass, Charbonneau's gun, all had disappeared.

"Stay where you are," Captain Clark shouted. "We'll wait out the storm. We can't go back. We'd drown in the mud. We'll have to climb out. There's a level place above us. I saw it yesterday when I was scouting."

97

The hail turned to snow. I crouched on the ledge, the baby in my lap. I closed my eyes and prayed to the Great Spirit. An eagle flew out of the sky, through the snow.

It was an omen. The snow ceased and the sun came out.

"Now we climb," Captain Clark said, "as fast as we can."

I took off my mantle, made a sling from it for the baby, and put him on my back. We went slowly, one slippery rock, one crevice, at a time. The sun grew hot and Meeko began to cry. I gave his foot a pinch to make him quiet down.

York was waiting for us. He had killed a prairie chicken with his tomahawk and put it to roast over a fire of buffalo chips, there being no wood in sight. Charbonneau dried off Meeko in front of the fire and gave him a chicken wing to suck on.

The sun was hot again as we started forth to circle the Great Falls. Soon the ground was steaming. By noon gnats fell upon us in clouds, digging at our eyes. To breathe we had to wrap nets around our heads.

The sun lured the rattlesnakes out of their winter lairs. They were squirming everywhere, as long as my arm. Scannon had been riding in a cart, but he was fascinated with Meeko. He jumped out and followed us until one of the rattlers struck him on the mouth.

His face swelled up to twice its size. His eyes disappeared. I helped him as much as I could. I made soup for him when we camped that night, though he could not swallow it. And Captain Clark gave him some of the same medicine he had given me.

In five days, Scannon was better. He began to eat. We had plenty of buffalo, so I fed him all he wanted, which was a lot. He could eat more than a hungry man. Captain Clark said that I had saved Scannon's life. This was not true, but afterward the dog did pay more attention to me than to anyone else, even his master.

I was so busy with Scannon I had not seen the Great Falls that Captain Clark had told me about. But I heard the sounds they made and felt the cold spray on my face. One dawn I stole away to the bluff and looked down.

Mist hid the river and the roar was louder than mountain thunder. When the sun rose, sparkling waters blinded me. I turned around to show Meeko, but he was too scared to look. When I got back to camp, Charbonneau hit me with a stick for not having his breakfast ready.

Yet I remembered the roar and the mist and the sparkling waters. I dreamed about them that night and thought about them the next day.

Wheels on two of our carts collapsed, being made of soft cottonwood, and we had to stop while the men made new ones. Carrion birds circled high above us and we were followed by flocks of chattering magpies. The wind was strong and made whistling sounds, sounds like curlews make. We were all very tired.

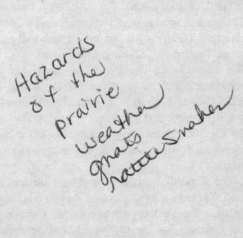

Hazards
of the
prairie
weather
gnats
rattle snakes

99

Chapter Nineteen

We reached the place above the falls that Captain Clark had marked with stakes and little flags. Here the canoes were put in the water, much to our delight, for the portage had been hard on everyone.

Clothes and food and all the provisions were loaded into the canoes. The men got out their ropes and poles and we went on toward the Shining Mountains.

The country had changed. The plains lay behind us. Great glittering rocks jutted out of the water. Dark cliffs towered above us, straight up from the riverbanks. The sky was a deep blue and far away.

On the second morning before we left camp, Captain Clark wrote down in his book and read to me what he had written.

" 'The fifteenth day of July, eighteen hundred and five,' " he said. " 'I have a strong feeling that on this day we will be in or near the land of the Shoshone. Captain Lewis has made sightings for the past week and he agrees.' "

He closed his book. "Do you see anything around you that looks at all familiar?" he asked me.

"Only the mountains with snow on them," I said. "Our

tribe moved around from place to place, but always near these snowy mountains."

"This is a good day for you to look for signs. It makes a big difference in what we do and which way we go. Do you want one of the men to take care of the baby?"

"He is no trouble. I will take him. We will watch for signs, both of us."

I saw nothing that day. But toward nightfall the next day, we came out of the deep canyon we had been struggling through, the men wading to their hips in the fast water, pulling the canoes. And I saw bits of thin smoke drift up from a grove of pine trees.

Captain Clark, Ben York, and I were walking on the shore, following the canoes. I told Captain Clark about the smoke.

"The fire was lit this morning. It is nearly out," I said. "If the tribe was still there the fire would not be dying. It is suppertime and they would have a big fire to cook by. They have seen us and think that we are enemies. The smoke may be a signal to warn their friends."

"Likely," Captain Clark said.

He was so sure they were somewhere near us that he left trinkets and pieces of clothing along the trail. I drew figures on the ground to show that we were friendly and tied bunches of grass to the trees to mark our direction.

For days the trail was the roughest we had ever traveled.

My feet got blistered and my eyes were nearly blinded from the gnats, but I was too excited to notice these things. At last I was in the land of the Shoshone, the beautiful land! My mother was dead, many of my friends were dead, all might be dead, even my father and brother Cameahwait. Yet I was happy, thinking of the long-ago times when we were all together.

I walked onshore with Captain Clark and Ben York, watching for signs of my people. I saw the print of a man's moccasin, a ring of cold ashes, wisps of smoke, a pointed quill that someone had lost. I walked so fast that York said I was killing him and begged me to walk slower. I was too excited to heed him.

We came to a deep ravine and had to leave the shore and travel on the river with the rest of the party. Here I saw no signs of my people.

Captain Clark gazed up at the dark yellow walls that rose on both sides of the river, at the blue sky high above us, where hawks and eagles soared.

"The Shoshone chose wild country to live in," he said. "The wildest and most beautiful I have ever seen."

"We did not choose the country," I said. "It was chosen for us. We were driven here by the Flatheads, by the Nez Percé and by the Gros Ventres and by others. We took shelter here from our enemies."

"Your enemies made you a fine gift," Captain Clark said. "It's a wondrous land."

The dark walls fell behind. We came out into country where the river ran shallow. Beaver dams were everywhere. In places they had to be cut away.

The round, blue stones that covered the river bottom tortured the men who towed the boats. Those who poled had to fasten hooks at the ends of their poles to keep them from slipping. It was a mighty task for the men to move the heavy canoes at all. To save weight, Captain Clark, Ben York, and I went ashore again and walked.

We circled green hills and a yellow bluff. We came out suddenly upon the river at a place where it divided and flowed left and right around a wooded island. It was the place where our tribe had camped, where I had picked berries on a sunny day, where the raiders had captured Running Deer and me, where my mother died.

I held the baby tight in my arms. I walked fast and did not stop until the island lay far behind.

I found Captain Clark and Captain Lewis with the canoes at a narrow bend in the river, held there by a beaver dam. I told them that I had just passed the island where I was stolen by the Minnetarees.

102

"You're certain?" Captain Clark said.

"Yes."

Later that day I heard the two men talking. Captain Lewis said, "Our Indian girl is certain she's in Shoshone country and has seen the place where she was captured. Yet she shows no emotion either of sorrow or of joy about it. If she has enough to eat and a few trinkets to wear she would be perfectly content anywhere, I do believe."

Little, oh so little, did he know about how I felt.

A week passed and we were in a wide meadow among rolling hills where the river had many loops and turns. I was in the canoe with Captain Clark and Ben York. The baby was in my lap. I had nursed him to sleep and was half asleep myself when a voice spoke to me.

The voice did not belong to the men. It might have been the wind speaking. Or the river speaking. Or my grand-father speaking. Whoever it was, I opened my eyes wide.

We were traveling through a heavy mist, against a fast current. There were white beaches along the shore and some green places where elk were grazing.

The sun rose and burned off the mist. I saw a broad valley where hills tumbled away to the mountain peaks, covered with snow.

I wanted to stand up to see better, but I had learned that you do not stand up in a canoe when it is moving in deep water or any kind of water. Instead, I got down on my knees.

We came to a bend. For a while the sun was in my eyes. Then the river straightened out, and not far away a great yellow bluff reared up in front of us. It was shaped like the head of a beaver. Jaws, nose, everything looked like a beaver.

"There," I said and pointed. "Look!"

Captain Clark was behind me in the canoe. "What?"

"Beaverhead."

"Beaverhead. What about it?"

"It is near the place where the Shoshone cross the mountains."

"To where the rivers flow the other way?"

"Yes. We came here to hunt buffalo in the summer."

"You're certain?" Captain Clark asked me.

"Yes."

Beaverhead was good news. The men with the poles and those with the long ropes broke into a song. Sergeant Ordway played his fiddle. It was the first song in many days.

"We'll take our time," Captain Clark said. "The Shoshone are out there all right, but they're scared. We'll give them a chance to see that we're friends."

He got out a red and blue and white flag and carried it. I painted my cheeks and the part in my hair with vermilion, the sign of peace. I even painted the baby's cheeks.

We saw a Shoshone signal fire beyond us on a peak and thought we saw a man on horseback moving through the trees. Captain Lewis decided to take George Drewyer and three hunters and go out to look for them.

I asked him if I could go along.

"It's dangerous," the captain said. "And you have a baby in your arms that needs nursing all the time."

"I have been through dangers before. Many times on this journey, Captain Lewis."

"This journey is far too dangerous."

"But the people you are going out to find are my people. They know me. They will welcome me. I can talk to them."

Captain Lewis fell silent. He had made up his mind that I would only be a nuisance. I said no more except to tell him how my people would be dressed and other things about them. I gave him one of my Shoshone charms, not the green stone, to show them. I said that if they thought he was a friend they would throw a blanket over his shoulders. They would rub their faces against his face. He would not like this because they would be covered with elk grease. But he must act happy and pleased.

He left us and rode up the river. We watched for him every day. We built big fires at night so he would know where we were if he came back. Many of our men doubted that he ever would. As for me, I was certain that he would find my people and they would all come back and meet us before we had gone far.

In the morning, two days later, before any of the men were awake, I got out of my blankets and went down to the river and bathed Meeko. The water was cold. He puckered his face but did not cry, because he had learned not to.

I laid him on his blanket—I had not found time to make another cradleboard—and gave him a hawk's feather to play with. With my feet deep in the sandy bottom, bracing against the swift current, breathless at the shock of icy water, I bathed myself and wrung out my hair. My tunic and moccasins were worn but clean.

The sun rose above the mountain, the Shoshone sun. As I had often before, long before the Minnetarees came, I knelt in the sand and prayed to the Great Spirit. I asked that my people, whoever was left, would be glad to see me after all these lost days. I was beside myself with joy.

But my joy did not last. As I took Meeko in my arms and left the river, Charbonneau came out of our tent. I had not built a fire yet. He glanced at the ashes and then at me.

"No fire," he said. "Shoshone swim. Shoshone fix hair. Fix trinkets. Look pretty. No fire."

I knelt down and fanned the ashes until I coaxed a spark out of them. I put some twigs on and fanned them alive and set branches on the burning twigs. Charbonneau watched me, pulling at his beard.

When I stood up, he took the baby. Without another word he struck me in the face with a backward sweep of his hand.

The blow sent me sprawling to my knees. I crouched by the fire, afraid to get up for fear of another blow. He broke off a branch and struck me on the back. As he raised the branch to strike me again, there was a loud noise and a leaping flame in the trees, and a bullet passed close above us.

Captain Clark stood beyond the tent, not far away, with

the rifle in one hand. With the other hand he dropped powder into the barrel and tamped it down. He swung the rifle up and glanced at Charbonneau, but said nothing.

Charbonneau did not look at Captain Clark or at the gun pointed at him, but he knew they were there. He tossed the branch into the fire and strolled down to the river, humming to himself.

As the sun came up, Captain Clark got the camp awake and we started off. The river ran swift, so ice-cold that the men's legs ached as they dragged the heavy canoes behind them. Beaver dams had to be cut away. Firewood was scarce, though green brush grew heavy along the banks. There was little to eat, a half meal each day. The men began to grumble.

On the seventh day they felt better. Near dawn we found four deerskins hanging on a tree, left there by Captain Lewis. At noon Captain Clark caught a glimpse of a horseman crossing the river ahead of us. Just a glimpse, and then he disappeared.

At the time we did not know that the horseman was a spy, sent by the Shoshone. Captain Lewis had found my people only a few days after he had left us, but the Shoshone doubted him when he said that Captain Clark and his men were coming up the river in canoes. They had sent the spy to see if he was telling the truth.

Three days after this happened, Captain Clark and Charbonneau and I set off on foot early in the morning. We had come to a meadow thick with cottonwood trees when I heard the neigh of a horse, then the sound of hoofs, then Shoshone voices shouting a Shoshone welcome, "Ah-hi-e, ah-hi-e!"

Two horsemen came out of the trees. I clutched Meeko. I ran and stumbled toward them. I sucked my fingers, saying with this sign, "You are from my tribe, the people who suckled me." The men sucked their fingers, too, and lifted me from the ground, baby and all.

Chapter Twenty

Women came out of the trees. A girl was among them. She had changed. She was not so slender as I remembered her and she walked slowly, with a limp. Could it be my cousin, Running Deer? Not until we were close, in each other's arms, was I certain.

"I thought you were dead. Many times I prayed for your spirit," I said to her. "But here you are, alive. And here among our people. How did you ever come this long way? How long did it take you? Were you hurt?"

Running Deer did not answer because I was squeezing the breath out of her. Not until Captain Clark came and took me by the arm did I let her go.

He took me across the meadow and through the trees to a lodge beside the river, a lean-to made of cottonwood saplings and hides. Inside it was dark, though a small fire was burning. It smelled of war paint and buffalo grease and warrior sweat. We sat down and took off our moccasins as proof of friendship.

A Shoshone chieftain was standing in the deep shadows at the back of the lodge. "We have a feeble fire," he said to one of the warriors. "Encourage it with a piece of your fat pine. It is not my wish to talk to people I cannot see."

His voice filled the lodge. It was shrill yet strong. I had heard it before, some time long ago. It reminded me of another voice, my father's voice. But it was not his.

The chieftain had fierce eyes and was tall and thin and wore a headband of eagle feathers. On his forehead was a yellow dot circled in red, which spoke of friendship and peace. His cheeks were painted with yellow sunbursts, which meant that a new day had dawned. In the dim light he looked like my father. Could this be?

The warrior placed a pine bough dripping with resin on the fire. The chieftain stepped forward out of the shadows into the light.

He looked taller in the light, much taller than my father. He cleared his throat to speak, but before he uttered a word, I saw at the corner of his mouth the scar I had given him once, the time we were playing together in the river. It was my brother, Cameahwait, He Who Never Walks.

Meeko was in my arms, but I hugged my brother anyway.

Charbonneau shouted at me so I gave him the baby, and my brother and I hugged each other again. I would have hugged him a third time except that he suddenly remembered that he was a Shoshone chief and a man. Chieftains and men do not hug women when other people are looking, and seldom at any other time.

I tried to speak but tears choked me. The tears would not stop.

My brother turned away and faced the white men and said a few words of welcome. He held a pipe hung with feathers, which was very tall and had a bowl made of bright green stone. He lit it with a hot coal and pointed the stem of the pipe toward the east, where the sun was, then to the sacred points of the world.

My brother held the pipe out to Captain Lewis, but before the captain could take it, he drew it back and repeated the ceremony three times.

He pointed the stem at the heavens, at the magic circle.

108

He drew on the pipe three times, puffed three times, then held it out for Captain Lewis, Captain Clark, and the other white men. At last he gave it to his warriors.

Captain Lewis stood up and told him why he had come. He said that he was on his way to a place called the sea, the great waters that were too salty to drink, and that he needed many horses to reach this far place.

"I know this place. We have shells from this place," my brother said. He frowned. "The Blackfeet came this year. They came in the spring and killed nine of our people and took women away and many horses. But we have many horses left and you can have what you wish of them."

Afterward, when they no longer needed me for the language, I went to look for Running Deer. As soon as I stepped outside a hand touched my shoulder.

I turned to find Man Who Smiles staring down at me, smiling his crooked little smile. He smiled crookedly all the time because a Blackfoot arrow had struck him when he was a boy and twisted his mouth.

"She has the black eyes of our people and the skin of the white people," he said.

He said this softly to Meeko as he leaned over and gave him a pat on the head. Meeko smiled because the man was smiling.

"This child is very pretty," he said. He gave Meeko a nip under the chin. Meeko gurgled and kicked. Captain Clark had spoiled him, the rest of the men had spoiled him, and Scannon had spoiled him too.

"I am going to steal this pretty little girl," Man Who Smiles said.

"The baby is not pretty," I said. "It is a handsome baby, not pretty. And he is a boy and not a girl."

"Ah-hi-e. A boy, of course. And how handsome he is. Someday he will break many hearts. Oh, yes."

The man touched both of Meeko's clenched fists. "Someday these hands will wield a mighty bow. They will send true arrows, kill many buffalo, slay the Great White Bear. What is your name, little one?"

Meeko did not answer. And I looked at Man Who Smiles and did not answer. I was trembling too much.

Once—long ago in another far place, it seemed—Man Who Smiles was young, three times my age, but young. He went to talk to my father and my father said yes, he could marry me, though he had two wives already. It was a promise my father had made to him and solemnly sealed. When twelve moons had risen and set, the marriage could take place.

Man Who Smiles gave back my gaze. His hair, which was now gray, was braided in a loop with porcupine quills and hung over one shoulder. He kept fingering the quills. He was nervous.

"What is the name of this one?" he asked.

"Jean Baptiste Charbonneau," I said.

"Charbonneau is the one with the hair on his face, and the eyes way back in his head that you can barely see? This Charbonneau is the boy's father?"

Women were gathering, standing off, but close enough to hear. Among them I saw three eager squaws who might be his wives.

"You, Sacagawea, are the mother," he said, smiling the smile that never faded. "You are the child's mother, yet by the law of our people, by the sacred law of the Shoshone, by your father's solemn promise, freely given, you belong to me. And the child belongs to me also. This is the law."

He had strong fingers. Before I could move, he snatched Meeko away. He grasped my hand. "Come," he said. "We will see Chief Cameahwait. We will talk. He will listen to me and give his consent."

My brother and the two captains were still in the lodge passing another peace pipe around. Charbonneau had left them. While we talked, he lounged in the doorway, listening to the Shoshone words, trying to understand what

110

we were saying. But when he saw Meeko snatched from my arms he ran toward us.

"You Indian, what happens?" he shouted. "What you do with baby?"

Man Who Smiles did not answer. He turned his back and strode into the lodge. Charbonneau followed him.

I could hear the baby crying. The women came closer. The wives of Man Who Smiles plucked at my sleeve and whispered advice.

The prettiest one said, "He is not a good husband. You will not like this one."

"He sleeps much," another said. "He does not hunt. When he is not sleeping, he eats."

"He eats much," the third wife said.

They edged up and fingered my blue bead belt and said they would like to have it. Would I trade it for some white antelope hides that would make a fine jacket? Behind them, Running Deer was watching. She was ready to help me if I needed her.

I ran into the lodge. Chief Cameahwait was asking Charbonneau for silence. "Sacagawea," he said, "is married to this one. She was married by the laws of the Minnetarees." He pointed at Charbonneau. "Before that, long before, she was promised by her father, by my father, to Man Who Smiles. A solemn promise, promised in true faith. I heard it promised by my father who is now dead."

The baby had begun to cry, so Man Who Smiles passed him to me. I turned Meeko right side up and gave him a breast to feed on. I was ready to tell both of the men and my brother and all of the women who were now crowded into the doorway that Meeko was mine. I would tell them that I would not give him up, no matter what was said and who said it.

Man Who Smiles stood holding a lance with a foxtail tied to it. Charbonneau had a hand on the hilt of his long-bladed knife. They did not look at each other, as if the other one was not there, but suddenly they were angry foes.

Someone warned Captain Clark of trouble. He came and stood between the two men. He looked sharply at me and said, "The choice is yours, Janey. Which man do you choose?"

My heart beat in my throat. Then I could not hear it beat at all.

"Choose," Captain Clark said. "We don't have days to make up our minds."

It is you that I choose. It is you that I love, were the words that I longed to say to him. But then I said, slowly, under my breath, "Toussaint Charbonneau."

The words fell like stones. Captain Clark knew they were stones. He knew how I felt about him.

Running Deer was waiting outside the lodge. She had not heard what I said to Captain Clark, yet she knew what I wanted to say. She had seen me walk into the camp that morning at his side. She had seen us go into the lodge together. She had watched when I had to choose between the two men.

Running Deer knew all this, but she said only, "You will kill yourself and your baby if you go on to the Big Lake. It is many, many sleeps away. None of our men have gone, but they have heard. They say that the mountains are high and the canyons deep and the rivers so fast that even the fish have trouble trying to swim."

Meeko began to whimper. She took him from me.

"What happened to his cradleboard?" she asked.

"It got lost in a storm."

"My baby died at the end of winter. It was a hard winter. We all went down the mountain, near the Great Falls, but still we found little to eat. That was when I lost my baby. I have her cradleboard if you would like it."

She took me to a small tipi of willow brush and hides, where she lived with her husband and his two other wives. He was asleep, so she was quiet with the cradleboard and did not give it to me until we were outside again. It was new and made of white birch. Meeko liked the blue-jay feathers that hung down from its top.

The sun was hot. We went and sat under a tree and did not talk for a long time.

Then Running Deer said, "You are going to the Big Lake because you love Captain Clark. You love the red hair and the blue eyes and the way he treats you. Also because he is a white man."

Her husband had come awake. He stood at the door of the tipi, holding his stomach. "I have three wives," he shouted. "But where are the wives? Where is the food? I guess I find myself two more wives, maybe three . . ."

Running Deer did not move or answer. "For this I will get a big beating," she said. "Does your husband beat you?"

"Sometimes."

"Big or small?"

"Both."

"What does he beat you with?"

"His fist, usually. Sometimes with a stick."

"Do you get used to it?"

"Never."

"I do, a little. If you married Captain Clark, would he beat you?"

"No."

"Why not?"

"He would never have to beat me."

"Shushu," Running Deer said, which means "good," but she said it as though she did not believe me.

Charbonneau came and stood over us. He glanced at the sun. "Time for eat," he said. "No food here anywhere. Shoshone eat sometime maybe?"

"Sometime," I said.

"Tomorrow, maybe," Running Deer said.

Chapter Twenty-one

preparing for over land journey

By nightfall clouds covered the sky. There was heavy ice on the ground the next morning and the wind blew hard. It was time to start on the long journey.

My brother, He Who Never Walks, gathered horses for us. The Blackfeet had stolen many from him, but he still had some seven hundred, and also some mules, he told me. He made a map on the ground for us, piling up sand in little mounds to show where the best passes through the Shining Mountains were, the mountains always covered with snow.

He drew a picture in the dust about the big river we were to follow. He said that he had heard from the Nez Percé, the Pierced Noses, that the river ran toward the setting sun and lost itself at last in the great lake of bad-tasting, evil-smelling water.

The canoes were buried at night, deep in the forest, so no one could find them. The blades of the canoe paddles were cut off to make pack-saddles for the horses. Packs were made of hides and filled with dried food, powder and ball, medicine and things that Captain Lewis had gathered after we left the Great Falls.

Chief Cameahwait did not wish me to go. "The river you

follow I have never seen," he said. "No Shoshone has seen it. But I have been warned. It is a wild river. A bad spirit rules it, the lord of its frightful waters and the dark canyons they race through. Do not go. You will be of no help. Stay among us and mind your baby."

"I have given my word to go," I said.

"Given it to the Great Spirit?"

"No."

"To what then?"

"I have given it," I said and dodged away from his question.

"To Captain Clark?"

I was silent.

"You follow a bad path, sister Sacagawea. It will bring you unhappiness."

With this warning loud in my ears I went to Running Deer. She was making a pair of moccasins for Ben York. I told her about my brother's warning.

"What will you do?" she asked.

"Go," I said. "But now I am going to the cave. Do you remember how we used to go there and talk to the Great Spirit?"

"I remember. We went in summer and other times too. And after I escaped from the Minnetarees, when I got home and was nearly dead from hunger I went to thank the Great Spirit."

"I am going, if only you will take care of Meeko."

"Yes, it would be dangerous with Meeko. Do you remember how we used to get lost? Once we were lost for three whole sleeps."

"Sometimes those days come again in my dreams."

I fed the baby and left him in her arms. I did not tell Charbonneau where I was going because he would laugh and forbid me to go. If I went anyway, I would get a beating when I got back, but it did not matter.

Beyond the camp where the river runs fast between

towering walls, there is a path that leads upward—not really a path, just handholds in the stone.

Along the trail to the place where the path begins, I picked up pebbles. Without them it is easy to get lost in the cave, as Running Dear and I did one time.

The sun was out but a cold wind blew. I had to climb hand over hand and pull myself up. The handholds were covered with ice. I went slowly, the bag of pebbles on my back. There is a broad ledge halfway up where pine trees grow. Here I stopped, built a fire, and broke off a branch from a pine tree and made a torch.

All kinds of snakes live in the cave, mostly rattlers. They come out late in the spring and warm themselves on the ledge. Then they crawl upward over a barren slope to the top of the mountain. At the first sign of winter they come down and lie around on the ledge for a few days.

Dozens of them were on the ledge. They lingered there as though they were sad to leave the sun and go into the cave and live in a dark world until spring came again. They did not bother me because I was careful not to bother them.

In the morning when the sun rises it shines far back into the mouth of the cave. Now the sun was overhead and I had to use the torch. The walls are black and shine with water that drips down from above. The ceiling shines too and is very low so you have to stoop.

At the first turn, where the path in the cave branched off in three directions, I took the farthest one to the right. At the next branch I left a pebble to mark the way because of the many twists and turnings that lay beyond.

After I had dropped nine pebbles I came to a small, three-cornered room. Crystals hung from the ceiling like spears and grew up from the floor like fat toadstools. Simile

The path led on but it was here that the Great Spirit dwelt. Here all the Shoshone had prayed since the day the first man and woman came up from the big cave below the cave, on the back of a mighty jewel-eyed serpent.

116

The walls were hung with buffalo and bear hides and the horns of deer and antelope. Between them were pictures of the sun and moon and stars and winds of the four directions. All were made of tiny pieces of mica.

I shone the torch on the walls. What a beautiful sight! It took my breath.

Water dripped from the ceiling in the center of the room and formed a small, clear pool. I put down the torch and washed my eyes, my mouth, my nostrils, and my ears.

Then I lay down on the stones and faced the north and stretched my arms wide. For a long time I thought of nothing. When a thought entered my mind I closed my eyes and pushed it away.

The room was quiet. All I could hear was the faint noise the torch made and the water dropping, one drop at a time.

When my heart was quiet, I said, "Great Creator, my name is Sacagawea. I hope you will remember that I was stolen by the Minnetarees and became a slave to these people. And that you heard my prayers and saved me from many dangers.

"Perhaps you forgot my prayers about Red Hawk, son of Chief Black Moccasin, because you never answered them. I forget things too. And maybe you have forgotten about Toussaint Charbonneau and how he won me in the Hand Game and I had to marry him. And you must know that it is not a good marriage if you have to marry someone you do not love. I did not love him then and I do not love him now."

Before, when I came here and prayed to the Great Spirit, I always made sure that he was listening before I told him why I had come. I made sure now that he was listening. I turned on my side and put my ear hard to the stone. I held my breath.

From below the stone, far beneath the cave and mountain, from the earth's throbbing heart I heard sounds. I heard

117

a stream, flowing gently through a meadow, making gay noises like children laughing.

Then the sounds changed. Now I heard a swift river, running between high black walls, over logs and dams and boulders in a torrent of thunder and fury. It was the many voices of the Great Spirit that I heard beneath me.

The sounds stopped, or seemed to. It was very quiet. The Great Spirit was listening.

I got to my knees and said quietly, "Please, ruler of the sun, moon, and the stars, of all the winds and the four directions, please grant my wish. I have more wishes, but this is the only one I truly wish. Turn his thoughts upon me, his smile and his love, and keep him safe on the long journey that lies before us. Please remember Meeko, too."

I listened for the sounds again, the furious river and the gentle stream in the meadow, the voice of the Great Spirit. I heard nothing. My torch died out and I had no way to light it. The place was suddenly dark. All I could hear was water dropping, one drop at a time.

Quickly I got to my feet and groped my way along the dank walls, out of the room. Where the turning should be I stopped and searched for the last pebble I had left when I came in.

I searched for a long time and at last found it. The next pebble I found much sooner. The third pebble, at a place where there were many turnings, I had trouble with.

The mouth of the cave was close. I could hear the wind blowing. But of the three turnings, only one would lead me out. The other two would take me deep into the mountain.

I got down on my knees once more. The pebble was not where I had left it. Something had come and brushed it aside. Or I had gone too far or not far enough. I crawled back and started over again. I searched in vain everywhere on the path and against each wall where the water was running.

I tried the turning on my right hand. I crawled until I

118

could hear the wind no longer. I crawled back and tried the left turning. This, too, led me away in the wrong direction. Then I found the rest of the pebbles. I stood up and put a hand out on each side of me and walked quickly into the daylight.

The sun was overhead, shining through the aspen trees. Snakes were still gathering at the mouth of the cave. Some were crawling up from below. Some were basking in the sun. Others were crawling into the cave.

I went down to the camp singing. I was certain that the Great Spirit had heard my prayer and I was hopeful that it would be granted to me. Meeko gurgled as I took him in my arms—he had never been left for so long a time before.

"You found the cave," Running Deer said. "And your face shows that you talked to the Great Spirit and that he listened."

"Ai!"

"What did you pray?"

Always I had told her what I prayed but this time I was careful. "About many things," I said.

"A safe journey to the big water that you cannot drink?"

"Oh, yes, about that lake."

"Whatever the Great Spirit decides, you and the baby should stay with me. I hear bad things about the country between us and the big lake. It is not good for babies."

Charbonneau had helped her take care of Meeko. He was standing off by himself, not listening to our chatter. But when he heard this last about his son he came and stood over us.

"Jean Baptiste Charbonneau stay here," he said. "Me stay. Sacagewea stay. All stay."

"You speak sense," Running Deer said.

Charbonneau nodded. "Shoshone girl's brother, he big chief. Ho. Big medicine, huh?"

I said nothing because it would do no good to argue. And I could not very well say that I loved Captain Clark, that I would follow him wherever he went.

Only Captain Clark could change Charbonneau's mind. I went in search of him and found him trying hard to talk to my brother. My brother told me that he wished to say something to Captain Clark. I said it with words and signs.

"Chief Cameahwait thinks you are a good man," I told Captain Clark. "Therefore he wishes to give you the name Chief Red Hair. He also wishes to give you his own name. But he will keep his war name, which is Black Gun. The names Chief Red Hair and Chief Cameahwait are yours. People of my own blanket will honor you forever."

My brother placed a tippet of ermine fur around Captain Clark's shoulders. The captain thanked him. When all this was done I told Captain Clark what Charbonneau had said.

"Do you want to go?" he asked me.

I nodded, not trusting myself to speak.

"I have asked you this before, twice before," Captain Clark said. "It's not too late. You're home now, among your own people. Think before you answer."

"I have thought."

"You will go?"

"Yes."

Everything had gone so well that Captain Clark decided to call our camp Camp Fortunate, and he put the name down in his journal.

Chapter Twenty-two

After Captain Clark talked to him, Charbonneau changed his mind. He decided that we would finish the journey, since there would be no pay for him unless we did.

Also, the captain told him to buy me a horse, a good horse, so I would not have to walk all the time. Charbonneau had a good one, but like all the men he thought that women and children should walk.

The canoes buried and the supplies packed on the saddles, we left my brother, Chief Black Gun. He had told us little about the country beyond, the big river and the Great Lake That Smelled, because he knew little. He had piled up pebbles on the ground and drawn things in the dust, but these were of little help to the captains.

On the second day of our journey, Captain Clark came upon an old man who belonged to the Shoshone tribe. His name was Petalashoroogalahat, Spotted Horse, and I translated what he had to say about the country to the west.

That night the captain wrote for a long time in his journal. Then he read me part of what he had written, I guess to make sure that I really understood what was before us in the many days to come.

"The old man told me," he said, "that for the first seven days we climb over steep and rocky mountains where we'll find no game to kill nor anything but roots to eat. The Indians are called Broken Moccasins. They live like bears among the rocks and feed on roots and berries and the flesh of horses they can steal from those passing by."

Captain Clark watched me as he read from the journal. We were sitting in the firelight, so I was very careful to see that my face did not change.

He read on. "The next part of the journey is through sandy desert, where the feet of our horses will give out. The pools of water, which exist here in the spring, will be dried up and we will perish of thirst."

He paused to let me say something. I was silent. My face did not change.

"The old man said that if we do live, we will still be far from the sea, the sea you call a lake, where there's a lot of water which no one can drink. His advice was for us to go no farther. To wait until spring, when he would be glad to be our guide to the big sea."

Captain Clark closed his journal. He put wood on the fire and stood looking down at me. He waited for a sign that I was frightened by what he had read.

"It sounds no worse than what we have been through," I told him. "It is different country but we have had bears, snakes, cactus, floods, storms, hunger, a mad beaver, a crazy buffalo, and more."

At the sound of my voice, Charbonneau, who had been asleep, stirred himself.

Captain Clark waited, looking down at me. He seemed unsure of how I felt. I grew suspicious. I had helped him reach the Shoshone camp, helped him make friends with my brother, helped him buy the horses he needed badly.

But after all this, was I no longer wanted? Were Meeko and I a burden now? An extra mouth to feed. A baby to worry about. Were we to be only a big trouble?

122

"You are telling all this just to frighten me," I said, raising my voice. "The old man made it up. He told you lies."

Captain Clark shook his head, as though he faced a rebellious child. "That's not the half of what the old man told me, as you well know. Do you wish to hear it again?"

I did not answer. I jumped to my feet and ran into the tent. I gathered up my blankets and all of my things. It was not a long walk back to the Shoshone camp, to my brother and Running Deer.

Captain Clark was standing at the door of the tent, barring my way. I pushed past him. As I did so the cradleboard struck him a blow on the chest, to which he replied with a loud groan. Suddenly, the next moment, he had me in his arms. He was kissing me. I could scarcely breathe.

He took the blankets and the things I had packed and went into the tent with them. Over his shoulder, he called back, "We go together, Janey, the three of us."

The descriptions of the land beyond the mountain that the old man, Spotted Horse, gave us were not half right. Not even close to what we found.

We never came to the land where there were pools of water, and these only in the spring. We found water everywhere—springs bubbling into rivulets, rivulets into brooks, brooks into streams, streams into rivers, and all this great flood of water rushing, rushing, down the mountains to the enormous water that Captain Clark called the sea and that the Shoshone called the Big Lake That Stinks.

One day we came to a Flathead village. We were given a haunch of deermeat, and Charbonneau wooed the chieftain's daughter. She was my age and had a pretty name, Alone in the Clouds. For a wedding gift he gave her father one of our horses. Fortunately for me, I did not have to put up with her on our way to the sea. She refused to go with him. Instead, she decided to wait until he came back.

From the Flathead village we rode into the worst country we had ever seen, so bad that it took us ten long days and long nights to get through it.

The ravines were narrow and strewn with fallen trees and slides of sharp rock that cut the horses' feet. One of the horses rolled down a bank and smashed the small desk that Captain Lewis used to write upon.

The weather was bad. Every day it snowed or rained. Our clothes never dried out. We were close to freezing though we built fires.

Worse yet, we found no game. No antelope or deer. The buffalo herds were far behind us. We starved and the horses starved. We had to eat twenty fat candles that Captain Lewis had stored away.

Before we got through the mountains, Captain Lewis put his desk together. He had counted eight kinds of pine trees as we went along. He sat down with the desk in his lap and put all their names down in his book.

We came out into open country. A river of white, churning water, the same river we had followed in the mountains, wound through it. It was called the Lochsa, which means "rough water."

Captain Clark and six hunters went on ahead. They happened upon a stray horse, which they killed. Half the meat they left for us. I had to eat it or see the baby starve.

A day later we came upon a large village of the Nez Percé, the ones whose noses were pierced by shells.

When I was a child I heard that they were friendly people, and this they proved to be. They gave us dried salmon, and their chieftain, Twisted Hair, smoked a peace pipe with Captain Lewis and Captain Clark.

I was no help with the talk that went on between them. I had never heard Nez Percé before, so Drewyer made his signs and they became good friends without words. Charbonneau was friendly, too, not with Chief Twisted Hair, but with the women. They were the prettiest women I had ever seen, with their glossy black hair and big eyes.

Most of our men were sick with the cramps, but Captain Lewis put them to work anyway.

Since the Nez Percé men were going up and down the river in canoes, he decided that we should go that way from now on. He sent the men into the forest and they came back with five big logs of yellow pine. These they shaped with hatchets and hollowed out with fire.

When the canoes were finished, he made a bargain with the Nez Percé to take care of our horses until the day we came back. Our saddles were buried in a deep hole, secretly at night, along with a keg of powder and a sack of rifle balls. Chief Twisted Hair gave us some baskets of camas-root flour and dried salmon.

With him as a guide, we started off from Camp Canoe in a misty dawn.

A crowd on foot and on horses moved along the banks, watching us float down the river. The women who were dressed in their finest clothes—antelope shirts decorated with small bits of brass cut into various shapes, their nostrils stuck through with pieces of shell as long as my finger—kept waving at Ben York, who had grown tired of all the attention.

"The women have made far too much over you," I said. The back of his hands had been rubbed raw by Shoshone and Nez Percé women trying to get the black off. "You are spoiled, Ben York."

"Not enough," he said, "not close to enough. But when I get back to St. Louis there'll be no rubbing to see if I am a white man painted black. I'll be black as a crow at midnight."

It was still raining. York had a deerskin flung over his head. He pulled it back and gave me a look.

"You're not black like I am," he said. "You're not white, either. Sort of in between, I'd say. In St. Louis they'll not be rubbing your hands to see if the black comes off. But they'll be curious. They see only a few Indian men and no Indian girls—at least, not pretty ones like you. They'll be admiring, saying nice things. But don't let this fool you. You're an Indian and I am a black man. I am a slave and so are you, in a way. If a white man marries you, he's called a squaw-man and people look down on him. The same as they'd look down on a white girl who married me."

York was watching from under his deerskin cape. He knew—now everyone must have known—that I loved Captain Clark. He was warning me. It was a clear warning, though it was given with a smile. It struck my heart like a stone-tipped arrow.

Chapter Twenty-three

Some Nez Percé men followed us down the Snake River as far as the rapids. They helped us greatly on the way, furnishing us with firewood for our cooking and some forty dogs for food.

The river swam with fish, so many you could almost walk from bank to bank and never touch the water. But they were dying, not good to eat. Chief Twisted Hair told us that the fish were salmon and that they came up the river from the sea to lay their eggs and then to perish.

The Nez Percé did not offer to guide us after we came to the rapids. They wanted us very much to spend the winter with them.

Captain Clark thought we should make a portage around the fast water. But Captain Lewis was against him, saying that there was no time if we wanted to get to the big lake before winter set in. Indians ran the rapids and so could we.

Captain Lewis was right. Four of our dugouts passed through. The fifth got caught on a rock, but with the help of some fishermen, it was pried free.

Farther on we came to very bad waters. Here the canoes were unloaded and carried, past three wooded isles, along a bank covered with aspen trees. Their leaves seem to turn round and round when the wind blows. I showed Meeko how they fluttered but he was too young to notice how beautiful they were.

We came to an island of fishing lodges. Thousands of salmon had been split and were drying on racks.

These people had a big vault about thirty strides long, made of dugout canoes leaning on a ridgepole. In the center of this high cave stood a great pile of human bones and at one end was a circle of grinning skulls.

All around the vault, things that had belonged to the dead hung from the ceiling—baskets, fishing nets, deerskins, and various kinds of trinkets. I saw the skeletons of many horses that had belonged to the dead and were sacrificed when their owners died.

Soon afterward we passed a chain of rapids strewn with huge black rocks.

We came to a village where men with pierced noses were fishing with gigs and the women were pounding dried salmon between stones. They put the powder in fishskin bags to sell at the mouth of the big river to the whites, we were told.

These people did not receive us kindly. I was lying down in the canoe, ill from the cold. Not until Captain Clark made me stand up, so they could see that I was a woman, did they offer him some of the powder they were making.

He bought seven plump dogs for food and a bundle of firewood, wood being scarce. The chieftain gave us a large bundle of horsemeat, but it was too old to eat.

On a cold morning soon after, we reached a plain and a broad green river, which Captain Clark said was the Columbia River. He was very excited.

That night a chieftain appeared with more than two hundred warriors beating on drums. They made a circle around us and sang.

Cruzatte played music on his fiddle and George Drewyer

made signs showing that we had come in friendship. Captain Lewis gave the leader a large medal with a picture of President Jefferson on one side. On the other side were a flag and an eagle.

We saw a high mountain covered with snow far off in the distance, which Captain Clark had heard was near the great waters. Birds I had never seen before—black ones called cormorants and big-billed ones called pelicans—flew around us.

The next day we saw a large canoe, three times the size of ours, paddled by ten men. The bow of the canoe swept up high in a pretty curve. It was carved in the shape of an eagle, the stern in the shape of a bear with black eyes and a red tongue. The men called to us in a language I had never heard before. The slurping sounds were like the ones you make when you pull your feet out of the mud.

Drewyer talked to their chieftain, Broken Face, making signs with his long arms and his big hands. Broken Face brought out a robe made of five beautiful skins. He wanted blue beads for it, a lot of them, two handfuls.

The robe shimmered in the sun. Captain Clark gazed at it. "Our supply of these beads is low. Make a bargain with something else," he said to George Drewyer. "I want the robe. I've never seen anything so beautiful in my life."

Drewyer tried to bargain with a gun and some powder, but the chieftain wanted beads, blue beads, a handful.

I was wearing the belt Captain Clark had given me. The chieftain pointed to it.

Captain Clark hesitated. Finally he said, "Do you mind if we trade him the belt?"

I minded terribly. Tears came to my eyes. But he had set his heart on the otter robe, so I took the belt off and gave it to him.

The river widened. I saw flocks of geese and ducks and more of the big-billed pelicans. The wind came out of the west and smelled of salt. Captain Clark said that the sea was close. Everybody cheered and paddled faster. When we camped Cruzatte got out his fiddle and the men danced.

We were camped on a sloping bank, up from the river. In the morning, water was lapping at my feet. Captain Clark said that there were tides in the sea. Its water flowed into the river twice each day. Twice each day it flowed out.

I drank some of the water, but only a little, remembering the bad things I had heard about it. They were all true. It tasted of bitter salt and fish.

That day the river widened some more. Cold mist hid the riverbanks and a north wind began to blow. Then rain came down hard. I did my best to keep the baby dry.

Toward dusk the rain stopped. Beautiful colors unfolded far out over the sea, though it was still hidden from us.

"We'll go there tomorrow," Captain Clark said. "By this time tomorrow you'll watch big waves beating on the shore."

We saw waves well before that. They came the next morning while we were moving along at a good rate in the middle of the river. There was no warning, no sounds like those we heard when we were near the rapids. Instead there was only the river, smooth as an antelope skin, stretching quietly toward the sea.

Right in front of us then, the river suddenly sprang up. I was covered with spray, salty and cold. The three of us kneeling in the canoe pitched forward. The baby screamed. Charbonneau, who could not swim, lay where he was and clutched the rail with both hands.

Captain Clark shouted for us not to move. To the four men who were paddling, he shouted, "Pull right, to shore. Pull hard!"

The men pulled hard on the big paddles, but the dugout did not move. It stayed where it was. Some big hand was holding it back.

I took the baby from the cradleboard and clutched him in my arms. Charbonneau yelled at me not to let go. His voice shook with fear. Captain Clark's fur cap had been blown away. His long hair swung wildly around his face. His face had turned white beneath his leathery skin.

The hand swept us backward. Now we were in a valley between two hills of churning water. For a moment I caught a glimpse of yellow sand and black rocks, the very bottom of the river itself.

In the next breath, the sand and rocks disappeared and we were lifted up, up, higher than the riverbank. We seemed to hang in the air for a long time deafened by thunderous sounds, the shrieks and moans of evil spirits.

Then it was very quiet. The mighty hand flung us aside and we were bobbing around against the bank. Captain Lewis and the rest of the men were well behind us, so they saw what had happened in time to reach the shore.

Waves of dark fog were facing in. I still clutched the baby in my arms. I could barely see him in the fog. He looked like a little ghost. Poor baby, poor Meeko!

We made camp in a grove of towering trees. It was hard to find anything dry enough to burn. Around a dismal fire the men talked about the happening on the river.

"The Columbia River flows out," Captain Lewis said, "and the sea flows in. River and sea clash. They fight to see who will win."

"Where did you hear all this?" Captain Clark asked him.

"I read it somewhere. In a journal. It happens twice every day."

Captain Clark was not pleased to know something he should have known before.

We were very close to the sea. All that night through the fog, I could hear it roar. The next morning, when Captain Clark crawled out of his lean-to, he asked me if I was glad that we had reached the sea.

"I heard it all night," I said. "And I hear it now. But where is it?"

"Beyond that far hill," he said.

He took a breath of the salty wind. He raised his hands to the sky. "The sea in view," he shouted. "In view, in view. Oh, the joy!"

He could not see the Great Waters. "How do you know that it is around the hill?" I said.

My words were lost in the pounding of the waves. I must have had a disappointed look on my face.

"I thought you would dance and sing with joy," he shouted. "Instead, you stand there like a lodgepole."

It was the first time he had criticized me. Tears leaped to my eyes. I turned and brushed them away.

He put his hand on Meeko's head. He pointed toward the Great Waters beyond the hill and said, "You see them, don't you, Pomp? Whether your mother can see them or not."

Meeko gurgled. He liked the sound of the name the captain used for him. Pomp! It made him kick at his cradleboard. The name sounded like an arrow striking a buffalo.

"Dry your tears," the captain said to me. "You'll stand beside the sea very soon."

"I would like to do that," I said. "We can walk up the hill and look at it now."

"Tomorrow," Captain Clark said. "Now we get out of the rain."

I did not stand beside the sea the next day. Or the next. Many days passed before I even caught a glimpse of it.

Chapter Twenty-four

The next day and the next we changed our camp three times. The thundering water kept the men awake at night, so we moved back two miles. Then the canoes were swamped by the tides in the bay where we camped. At the third camp, wood and water were scarce. Captain Clark named the place Cape Disappointment.

Of all our troubles, rain was the worst. It rained night and day, gently or hard. It never stopped. Our clothes, our moccasins, our blankets, which were worn from the long journey, began to rot, and we had no hides to make new ones.

Some of our troubles were the natives. They called themselves Clatsops. When they were babies their mothers put their heads between two boards. In this way as they grew up their faces widened and their heads flattened so that their heads and foreheads were in a straight line. It made me shudder to think of Meeko's head flattened out between two boards.

Clatsops dressed in strange clothes. Captain Clark said that they had bought the clothes from the white men who sailed up and down the shore in ships many times larger than our largest canoe. The Clatsops traded otter pelts for coats that did not fit, satin breeches too long for their legs, wool hats too big or too small for their heads.

They stole things right under your nose, while you were looking at them. They were greedy besides. Captain Clark offered one of them his watch, a handkerchief, a bunch of red beads, and a piece of silver money—all of these things for one otter skin. The man shook his head. He wanted also a handful of blue beads.

Captain Clark told him to leave the camp and not come back. The man and his wife left but on the way the wife picked up a tomahawk. They ran into the woods and hid.

Captain Clark went looking for them but never found them. When he came back he was out of breath but not angry. He said, "They've been trading with men from the American ships and learned some of their tricks. I don't blame them too much."

We moved from this camp because game was scarce and hordes of fleas lived in our blankets. Before we moved, Captain Clark carved some words on a pine tree.

First, he chopped the thick bark away with a hatchet. Then he drew the words with a piece of charcoal on the clean place he had made. With a knife he carved out the words. It took him a long time. When he was done, I asked him what the words said.

" 'William Clark, December 3rd 1805. By land from U. States in 1804 & 1805,' " he read, very pleased with himself.

He held out his hands. They were covered with blisters.

"I would carve your name if I could hold the knife any longer," he said. "You came, too, all the way from Fort Mandan. Aren't you proud of yourself?"

I did not answer. Was *he* proud of me? That was all that mattered in the world.

"We could never have done it without you, Janey," he said.

My heart beat loud enough to hear.

"Your name belongs there, right beside mine," he said and kissed me.

That night when everyone was asleep I found the knife and a candle and went to the pine tree. The first word he had taught me to write was my name. There was a space just below everything he had carved. In it, by the light of the candle, I chopped out the word "Janey" as best I could.

In the morning light it looked crude, not so nice as the words he had carved out, yet it could be read. I doubt that he ever knew about it, for we moved that day. But I knew that my name was there beside his.

We moved across the river to a place the men had built. It was called Fort Clatsop. A stockade sixteen strides square, it had three cabins facing four cabins and an open space between them.

Life was better here. Our clothes got a chance to dry out and there were fewer fleas and mosquitoes. But food was still scarce, though our hunters went out every day.

For a long time we mostly ate the same things as the Clatsops ate—roots of the fern, rush, sweet licorice, and thistle. The men caught a beaver in their traps, and we feasted on fat beaver tail. I chewed up a piece and fed it to Meeko. He liked it as much as I did; he smiled, wanting more.

A friendly Clatsop and his four wives came to the fort and brought us a basket filled with the fat of an enormous fish. A fish as big as the fort had perished on the shore nearby. Our men thought this fish tasted like dogmeat. Not having tasted dogmeat I cannot say.

The captains decided to go down to the shore with some of their men and bring back a load of fat. I wanted to see this enormous fish very much.

Besides, since we reached the mouth of the river I had never laid my eyes on the sea. The men had talked about it since the day we left the Minnetarees. I had almost drowned in the waves the sea made. I had heard it and smelled it. But never in all those days had I stood and looked at the sea and shown it to my baby.

I asked if I could go with them. Captain Lewis eyed the cradleboard on my back.

"You and the baby?" he said.

"I can leave the baby with his father."

Charbonneau had told me already that he was not going to go on a long walk and carry a heavy load of fish fat around on his back.

"They not hired Charbonneau for carry fat," he said. "Hire him for guide. Anyhow, Charbonneau's feet, they have more blisters than toes."

Captain Lewis said, "Your husband and I have had a talk. He's decided to go with us. So you can't leave the baby with him."

"I can carry the baby," I said. "I have carried him for many sleeps. From far away, from Fort Mandan to this place."

Captain Clark said, "Come! I'll carry Pomp."

I gave him the baby and the cradleboard, which he strapped to his back, and we started off. We climbed to the top of a high hill. I could hear waves pounding on the shore. The Big Water, the Great Water, the sea, lay below us, but I could not find it because of the mist.

Clatsops had made a trail to the shore, but it was very steep and we had to hold on to bushes as we went down one step at a time. We met a band of Clatsops coming up from the shore with loads on their backs.

We came to a wide, sandy shore, much like the shores along the Missouri River, except the sand was much whiter. I stopped and peered, looking for the big sea. I saw nothing except swirling mist, but as I walked farther down the shore, water curled up around my legs and drew back. Then more water came up and drew back.

"At last, here's the sea you've heard about. How does it feel?" Captain Clark asked me.

"Very cold," I said and took a mouthful.

"How does it taste?"

"Very bad," I said, getting rid of it.

"The tide runs in and it runs out."

"Out where?"

"Around the world."

"World? That's a new word for me. I have never heard 'world' before. What does it mean?"

"It means the place where we live. Here. All around us. And beyond. The streams and rivers, hills and mountains, meadows and prairies, the Great Lake, the sea that lies before you, and many other seas just like it beyond here. The world is round just like a prickly pear and it spins like the tops children play with."

My head spun too. I saw a picture of the land and the streams and the rivers, the big waters, the seas going on and on. But I could not see these things, all of them, in a round ball like a prickly pear spinning round and round.

Sun broke through the mist. I saw rocks covered with brown weeds. Water washed over them and the weeds trailed out and glistened. Among the weeds were animals lying on their backs.

"Sea otter," Captain Clark said. "The Clatsops kill them and sell their pelts to the white traders."

Beyond the rocks, fish were swimming about, diving and coming up. They were blue and flashed in the sun. I asked Captain Clark what kind of fish acted like that, like children playing a game.

"Dolphins," he said. "They are not fish, I'm told by Captain Lewis. And they don't have fur, so the Indians don't kill them."

Tired of answering my questions and fearing more, I guess, he handed me the cradleboard, turned away, ran down the beach, and disappeared.

Water was washing against my legs. I scooped up some of it and washed my face and Meeko's face. Then I took him out of the cradleboard and let him stumble around in the water, which he tried to drink.

I raised my hands. I said a prayer to the Great Spirit who ruled over everything. Over the Great Sea that went on and on forever, over the world that spun and spun.

The chieftain we passed on the trail had stopped with his women halfway up the cliff. He pointed up the beach to let me know where Captain Clark was and called down a jumble of Clatsop words. The women put down their baskets. The chieftain called again. The women picked up their baskets, the chieftain waved, and they all went up the trail laughing.

I should have known from their laughter what I would find.

When I followed Captain Clark's tracks around a bend, I found him and his men staring at a strange sight. It was as huge as a long house. It looked like a chieftain's house that is just being built, when only the bare poles show.

It was the enormous fish. The Clatsops had stripped it clean. Only bones and a great gaping jaw were left.

All the camp looked toward a day they called "Christmas." Christmas morning there were songs and shots from the cannon, and twelve twists of tobacco were divided. But we had little to feast on, just some spoiled elk, pounded fish, and small helpings of a black root the Clatsops said was shan-na-tah-que. That night Drewyer sat by the fire and told stories about what he had seen and done.

Some of them were hard to believe, like the story about the time he was riding down among the Spanish peaks in the winter, where it had snowed for eighty days and in most places the snow was eighty feet deep.

"I was riding along over the treetops," he said, "and after a while I came to a canyon where there wasn't any snow, and when I crossed over to the other side I came to a valley where grass was growing green and there were green leaves on the trees."

His face was serious.

"It seemed like a good place to camp," he went on, still looking serious. "I was hungry. Sitting up on the limb of a tree, I saw a fat partridge, so I brought up my gun and shot him right through the eye. The bird fell off the limb and broke into a dozen pieces. Fell in the grass and the grass broke into pieces. I went down to the stream to drink and the water was stone. I saw some raspberries growing, but I broke my teeth when I went to eat them—they were rubies. I thought I would make a fire and got out my ax and chopped on a log. But the log was hard, like the water, and I smashed the ax. I was in a stone forest, for certain."

"What did you do with the rubies?" Sergeant Ordway asked.

"Gave them to some Spanish girls," Drewyer said. "I was young and foolish in those days. Wish I had the rubies now. They were as big as plums."

Captain Clark smiled. "Big as plums?"

"Bigger," Drewyer said, his face still serious. "And a sack full up, right to the top."

The men laughed, but I didn't. I wondered if there could be such a place somewhere in the Spanish peaks. I thought of the great waters that went on and on around the world, and the mountain cave where the Great Spirit dwelt, and other things, too.

Chapter Twenty-five

The chief of the Clatsops and his wives came to the fort a few days later with jugs of elk fat. He asked double what they were worth—a string of the precious blue beads.

He was sent away but in a week he returned. This time his wives brought five canoes. The canoes were so light that the women carried them in one hand. For these he asked three strings of the blue beads and also Captain Clark's deerskin pants.

The captain did not mind trading his pants for canoes that would be helpful on the many portages to the Shining Mountains and across them to the Missouri and Fort Mandan. But three strings of blue beads were too much to pay. Besides, he had only one string of the blue beads left.

"By chance," he said to me, "do you have any blue beads hidden away somewhere? A canoe that's so light one person can carry it would be a big help on the way back to Fort Mandan."

I felt disappointed that we were getting ready to leave. I still wondered why we had come so far and everyone had struggled and suffered so much, just to turn around and go back so soon.

More than this, I wondered about Fort Mandan. What would happen to me when we got there?

"If you have a few beads, just a few, I can make a bargain," Captain Clark said.

"I have white beads."

"No blue ones?"

"None."

"Perhaps you have another belt like the one you gave me, the one we traded for the otterskin robe?"

I said nothing. I had not given him the belt. He had taken it from me. *We* had not traded the belt, *he* had traded the belt. Firelight was shining in my face. He must have seen my tears. He must know that the hurt I felt when he traded my belt away was still in my heart.

"I know you hated to make the trade," he said.

"You gave the belt to me," I said. "It was mine."

"I know, I know, but otter is the most beautiful fur in the world. And these were the most beautiful pelts I had ever seen, so beautiful they reminded me of a story I heard once. Would you like to hear it?"

I was silent, just to let him know that I did not care what he said.

He told the story anyway. "Far on the other side of the world," he said, "high in the mountains, in a place called Tibet, the women make wonderful shawls. These shawls are made of shatoosh, which looks like wool. It seems just like wool until you touch it. Then you feel as if you were putting your hand in a cloud."

I remembered how I had gasped when the chieftain held the furs up to the sun. How I had wanted to put them around my shoulders! But I had prized the belt much more because he had given it to me.

"Shatoosh comes from the wool of the wild goats that roam the peaks," Captain Clark went on, "goats like the white-tailed antelope you know about. These Tibetan goats are not shorn. Women and children collect the wool from thorns and trees and stony ledges where the goats have snagged themselves. From these hairs they weave shawls so fine that they can be pulled through a loop as small as the ring on my finger."

He held his hand out to show me his ring. It had a blue stone that was shaped like a heart. I had seen stones like it before. They came from people far to the south who call themselves Navajos.

Captain Clark took the ring off and told me to put my hand out. He put the ring on my finger.

"The ring is not so beautiful as the belt of blue beads," he said, kissing the finger that had the ring on it. "But always when you look at the ring, it will remind you of our journey together."

I could not wear the ring in front of Charbonneau, so when he came back from a game boasting that he had won a knife with an ivory handle, I hid it away.

The Clatsop chief returned in the morning with his many wives. They had a big black canoe instead of the five light ones, which he would sell for beads of any color, also an ax, two knives, ten fishhooks—half big, half small—and our air gun.

The canoe had fine carvings at its stern and bow and could carry a heavy load. Captain Clark wanted it badly, but the gun belonged to Captain Lewis, who would not part with it.

"Knives, ax, hooks, beads," Captain Clark said. "No more."

"Muckamuck," the chieftain said. "Nothing."

"Your black canoe leaks," Captain Clark said. "There's a hole in it somewhere."

"Gun has no powder," the chieftain said.

Captain Clark thought. Then he went off and came back with a gun. He filled it with powder, twice as much as usual, and gave it to the chieftain. The chieftain had porcupine quills braided in his hair. When he pressed the trigger, there was a great shaking and the quills flew out in all directions.

He liked the noise so much that he forgot about the air gun, handed over the black canoe, and made us a gift of some old elk tallow.

We were pleased with the gift. I boiled the tallow and spent the rest of the day making candles. By nightfall I had poured more than fifty, fat and two hands tall.

During the winter we had been busy dressing deerskins. There was a good supply of clothes for all our men as well as dozens of good moccasins, enough to last until we reached Fort Mandan.

We also collected roots and smoked as much meat as we could spare, knowing that the salmon fish would not come up the river to lay their eggs until weeks after we started. This meant that the tribes from here to the big mountains were hungry and we could expect to buy little food from them.

Our big problem was the lack of things to trade for dogs and horses. We had six blue robes, one scarlet robe, five robes made of a red, white, and blue flag, and a few tattered clothes trimmed with ribbon. That was all we had left. We had no beads of any color to trade with.

Soon after we started up the river we came to a village of Neerchokioos. Here the lack of trading goods led to our first trouble. The Neerchokioos had a supply of roots but did not like any of the things Captain Clark offered them.

They were a sullen, unfriendly lot and we thought that they might attack us. Captain Clark solved the problem.

He sat down by the fire in front of the chieftain and his warriors. He threw some powder into the fire, took out a pocket compass, and with his magnet made the needle turn round and round. The fire flared up violently and cast a strange red glow.

Women screamed. Children ran to their beds and covered themselves with hides. The chieftain tried to look brave but jumped up, laid a big packet of wappatoo roots at Captain Clark's feet, and begged the captain to kill the monster fire.

On the river soon afterward, a Wahcellah chieftain and six of his men appeared in camp at dusk. He admired Scannon. He walked around eyeing him. He had never seen a dog as big as a buffalo.

He sent four of his men away and they came back with four beautiful beaver skins, which he offered to trade for the dog. Captain Lewis thought for a while but refused the trade.

The chieftain was angry. Early the next morning, while the camp was asleep, he stole in with his men and lured Scannon away, possibly with a fish, since this was Scannon's favorite food.

The thieves had not gone far before we discovered that the dog was missing. The camp was in a fury. Scannon was more than a pet. He had saved us from prowling bears and a buffalo that stampeded us. He had caught birds and squirrels for Captain Lewis's dinner. He was our hero.

We were camped in a forest in a rough country where horses had to pick their way. York ran fast, so Captain Clark sent him out on foot with three horsemen to follow their tracks and bring the dog back.

Men stopped eating, picked up their rifles, and got ready to pursue the thieves if York and the horsemen failed. We waited for a long time. We did not know what would happen.

But things turned out well. York overtook the thieves and came back, riding an Indian horse, followed by Scannon and two of the Wahcellahs' dogs.

"The thieves," York said, "six or seven of them, were standing out in front of a big tipi, feeding Scannon strips of buffalo meat. I let out a war whoop and waved my tomahawk. For a moment they stared at me, their faces pale as a fish's belly. The next moment, before I could whoop again, they were gone. Vanished as if they had never been."

We had no better treatment farther along the river. At supper, when we invited the Weocksockwillacums, one of their young braves became angry at Captain Lewis for eating a piece of roasted dog. The Weocksockwillacums did not eat dog, so the young man showed his disgust by tossing a puppy into the captain's plate. The captain seized the puppy and threw it back.

None of these first villages was as friendly as they had been when we went down the river. Captain Lewis thought it was because we were out of trading goods. Captain Clark thought the people were unfriendly because they had endured a long winter and were hungry. Charbonneau thought both of them were wrong.

"They fear white mens because gods speak," Charbonneau said. "Gods tell them, 'Look out, Indian. White mens take fish, horses, land, water. Everything. In eye-wink, gone. Goodbye!'"

Not until we came upon the Skilloots did we fare any better. The whole village was wild with joy. They had caught a salmon that day, the first of the spring, a silver-scaled, pink-fleshed fish as long as my arm.

They knew from finding the salmon that vast schools were coming. To bring them soon, the people cleaned the fish, cut it into small pieces, and gave a piece to each child in the village. Because of their great joy, Captain Clark was able to get six dogs from the Skilloots.

He tried to be friendly with all of the people we passed on our way up the river. He waved to them, cupped his hands, and shouted to them in whatever words came to his mind. He waved whether they waved or not.

Whenever we came to a village where there were sick people, he did his best to heal them. He was very good with his medicines and very patient with everyone, old and young alike. He was pleased when someone who had been sick for weeks got well in a day or two.

He worked over Meeko when the baby was deathly sick.

Meeko had left Fort Clatsop with a bad cold that he caught from the rain. He was almost over the cold when he got a bad place under his ear. The place turned red and swelled out. Meeko burned with fever. Everyone thought he was going to die, everyone except Captain Clark.

He made a sling so I could carry Meeko around my shoulder and watch him better than if he was in the cradleboard.

He made a poultice of wild onions and put it on the swelling. When it did no good, he gave the baby a white powder mixed in water. When this did no good, he tried a salve of beeswax and resin, pitch and bear's oil.

I was too worried to eat, but he forced me to.

Charbonneau was worried also. He made a bandage of beaver fur and elk grease, which the captain would not let him use. Sometimes Captain Clark cradled the baby in his arms and sang to him.

I think it was his singing that got Meeko well.

I watched him save the baby. I had heard him joke with the men, those who waded over the sharp stones in the icy water. In the bad places I had seen him tie a cord around his waist and help the men pull the heavy canoes. I had watched him sweat in the sun and douse his head in the water to cool himself off. I had watched him comb his red hair dry so that it shone like copper.

When Meeko got well again, I watched him toss the baby high and speak silly words. Seeing them together was my life.

Chapter Twenty-six

We came to the Shining Mountains. Behind us were the Columbia River and the sea. Ahead of us were the Yellowstone River and the Missouri. It was summer, yet snow lay deep on the trail.

I rode a black horse that Captain Clark had bought for me from the Nez Percé. It was much easier riding in the snow than lower down where it had turned to slush. When we went over the mountains before, Meeko had been too young to enjoy the snow. Now when we camped I let him loose to stumble around in the drifts with Scannon nosing around at his side.

We had enough horses to carry our men, all their baggage, and all the things Captain Lewis had collected. But when we had gone through Lolo Pass on our way to the sea it was clear of snow. Now the snow lay heavy and had covered up all the landmarks. The Pierced Noses said that game would be scarce and the horses would be without grass for several days.

Yet the captains decided to move. If we waited, there would be no chance to reach Fort Mandan that year. We would eat no more than one meal each day. The horses could go without grass, the captains thought. Two of the Nez Percé promised to overtake us before we went far.

We moved into Lolo Pass on snow twice the height of our horses. The guides did not come. We suffered from the cold. I wrapped Meeko in two blankets. There was no game, not a bird bigger than a wren. The horses found no grass.

Drewyer, our only guide, wondered if we were on the right trail. The captains said we must be lost, so they gave orders to turn back.

The men dug pits in the deep snow and buried what little food we had, all the baggage, and all the papers the captains had kept. Drewyer hurried ahead to see if he could find a guide in the Nez Percé village we had left only a few days before. He was told to offer a fine rifle to anyone who could lead us as far as Traveler's Rest.

We pressed on behind Drewyer, numb with cold. There were many frozen toes and fingers and faces. Trouble dogged us from the start. We lost a valuable mule and four horses. One of the men cut a vein in his leg. Captain Lewis could barely stop the bleeding. Another of the men tumbled with his horse while crossing Hungry Creek and lost his only blanket.

After three days without grass, the horses began to starve. I cut long strips from the bark of an alder tree and fed them to my horse as we went along. The horses gnawed at each other's tails. By the time we came to the Nez Percé village, their tails were nothing but nubs.

We found guides in the village. The brother of Chief Cut Nose and two young warriors for the gift of two rifles agreed to show us the way over the pass. Captain Clark discovered some blue beads he had forgotten and bought salmon with them.

We started back at once in the fierce cold. In two days we reached the place where our goods were buried and dug them up.

There was little to eat, nothing for the horses. The guides brought us to a lofty crag where the Nez Percé had built a stone mound and put up a pole. It was a sacred place for them. They said that just beyond we would find food for our starving horses.

They were right. The next day we came to vast fields of grass. The day after that we were out of the heavy snow. Then came a blissful sight. Our hunters who had gone on ahead of us had killed a deer. The carcass lay beside the trail, ready to eat.

That night Captain Lewis spoke to us while we ate our first meal in days. We were camped near a village of Flatheads.

"In the winter, Captain Clark and I decided to look for a shorter trail to the Great Falls," he said. "We'll go with two parties. I'll take a party up the Hellgate and Blackfoot to the falls. Then I'll explore the River That Scolds at All the Others and try to find out if there's a river that flows into it from the north country."

Captain Lewis was serious. He repeated his words again and named those men he would take.

"This is very important," he said. "One of the reasons we made this journey was to find such a river. If it does exist, we will have a quick, sure way to carry Canadian furs down to the Missouri and hence to market."

He went on, speaking slowly. "Captain Clark," he said, "will take a party to the forks of the Beaverhead, where our boats were left last fall. After the boats are put in condition, he will choose men to take them to the Great Falls. In the meantime, I will have left men there and the two parties then will carry everything on a portage around the falls."

The talk went on for a long time, but after I heard that I was to go with Captain Clark, I did not listen. I thought about Running Deer and my brother and all the Shoshone people. We were close to the place they always camped late in the summer, but now they would be down below hunting buffalo, too far away for us to see them again. I would never see them again. I also thought about Charbonneau's new wife, the girl he had chosen from the Flathead village.

That night I said to him, "We are close to the place where you left your Flathead girl. Tomorrow we go with Captain Clark in a different way. You do not wish to spend days riding back to find her."

I hoped with all my heart that he would go and find the girl and somehow decide to stay with her and the Flatheads. Not a day had gone since we left Fort Clatsop that he had not complained about his health—the blisters on his hands from paddling, his saddle sores, his cough. Or the long way he now had to travel to reach Fort Mandan. Or how much he disliked Captain Clark.

"You had best go now," I said. "Not someday."

He grunted. "Ho! Charbonneau forgot. Bad husband, Charbonneau, huh?"

"Just forgetful," I said. I did not wish to cause trouble.

"Maybe Charbonneau should go now. What you think, Shoshone?"

"Go," I said. "Your wife may have a baby."

"Sure. Two babies, huh? Charbonneau great man, huh?"

But in the morning he had forgotten about his Flathead wife. We were on the trail two days before he spoke about her again. He got up from the breakfast fire and wiped the deer tallow from his beard. Everyone was asleep. He spoke quietly under his breath.

"Charbonneau go now. Shoshone go too. Hurry. Keep little mouth closed. Shoshone mouth also."

"Go alone," I said. "It is a long way to the Flathead village, and a longer way back because by then Captain Clark will be five or six days ahead of us. We do not know the trail. We may never catch up with him. We may get lost."

"Ki yi! Captain Clark, Captain Clark, he is not your husband. Lost? Zut!"

I was kneeling by the fire, scooping dirt to put it out. I said nothing more and went on with the dirt. The horses were tied close to the tent lest they be stolen in the night. He untied two horses. He picked up Meeko, who was asleep beside me, and put him in the cradleboard.

I still knelt by the fire. When I did not move, he yanked me to my feet.

"Hurry," he said. "Charbonneau not want nobody to see. Nobody's business, huh?"

Meeko began to cry. I did nothing to stop him. I put the cradleboard on my back, taking my time, and did not get on the horse. I walked slowly around the fire, away from Charbonneau, then ran toward our tent.

He caught me before I had gone far, caught the cradleboard and wrenched it from my back.

He put a hand on my throat. "Quiet," he said, "or Charbonneau make you quiet. For a long time, quiet."

"I must nurse the baby," I said with all the breath I had. "He will die if he is not nursed."

"Charbonneau will find good food for Jean Baptiste. Buffalo, deer, antelope, good thing all the time."

He tightened the grip on my throat. "You come, Shoshone?"

Our talk had awakened some birds. There was no sound from the camp, but a candle burned in Captain Clark's tent.

"Now, Shoshone, you come?"

"Yes," I said, with the last of my breath.

He helped me into the saddle and climbed into his. Quietly we rode out of camp toward the trail we had come along the day before. When we were out of hearing, Charbonneau gave me the cradleboard and the baby. He kicked his horse into a quick trot and shouted for me to follow.

I followed him for a way until we came to a stream. It ran deep with swift water from the melting snow. I knew it from my childhood. Farther down, it made a wide pool and I had bathed there with my cousin, Running Deer.

The day before when we crossed the stream, we had had a hard time. One of the men was thrown into the water and would have drowned if Ben York had not saved him.

Now, as Charbonneau got to the deepest part of the stream, when his horse had to swim, I turned back. There was a short cut to our camp which I knew about. I took it and rode fast.

The camp was awake and fires were burning. I startled Captain Clark as I rode up. He was angry when I told him what had happened. He wanted to go after Charbonneau and bring him back. York wanted to go, too.

"We'll make him walk," York said.

"He'd never get here," Captain Clark said. "Not walking on the feet he complains about all the time."

"He will find his wife and come back. He is very worried about her," I lied. Again with all my heart I hoped that he would stay with her and the Flatheads.

Five days later he rode into camp. We were camped in a village on the Yellowstone. The people there were glad to see us, even before Captain Clark gave them the last of our ribbons and some silver buttons from an old coat.

At one side of the village was a grove of fir trees. Fir has many dry branches near the ground and throughout the whole tree. To welcome us and bring fair weather on our journey, the people had set them ablaze. Each tree was a sputtering spire that flared from top to bottom.

On this night Charbonneau and his Flathead wife and her two slaves rode into the village. In the blazing light she looked beautiful. In the morning, when I cooked breakfast for her, she looked even more beautiful.

It was very cold. A wind blew down from the snowy peaks and we were surrounded by heavy drifts of snow.

She wore white moccasins that were sewn with blue beads and little bunches of porcupine quills. Her white ermine jacket had a circlet of black weasel tails around the collar.

The breakfast fire shone on her face, which was shaped like a heart. She was the daughter of a chieftain. She looked like a chieftain's daughter.

She acted like one, too. The camas root I baked for her she did not like. It had been dug long before it was ripe, she said. The elk was stringy. She had a pretty voice. It sounded like a rivulet running over a bed of ferns.

Charbonneau could not keep his eyes off her. He sat and listened to her babbling, mostly about how powerful her father was. Charbonneau listened with his mouth open wide.

She had the finest horse I had ever seen, yellow with orange spots. Her saddle was lined with brown beaver fur. That night, while we were asleep, she got into her beaver-lined saddle and rode away on her fine horse with her two slaves.

I urged Charbonneau to go and bring her back. "It is a law," I said. "The Minnetarees and the Blackfeet and the Shoshone say that you can make her come back. You can kill her if you wish."

He expected me to be jealous. I was not.

He muttered and tore at his beard, yet he was afraid to go. "I like this Shoshone better," he said and threw his arms around me.

But the next day, while we traveled through Big Hole Valley, where I knew the trails and streams and could be of help, he was angry. Whenever I told Captain Clark what trail to take, Charbonneau would wait until no one was watching, then give me a slap.

Captain Clark was not sure of the country. It all looked alike to him. But not to me. I remembered Shoshone Cove from the way the cottonwoods grew on a little island. And I told him that soon we would come to a gap in the mountain where we would find the canoes we had hidden the year before.

By good fortune I was right. We reached the gap and found the canoes in the river where we had sunk them. We also found the supplies we had left. The pounded meat and berries were still good.

It was the chewing tobacco that the men were most glad to see. They had been chewing tree bark mixed with dry leaves, kinnikinnick, for weeks. They chewed and chewed and spat and spat all day while they searched for a second lot hidden the year before. The chewers never found it. "An awful loss," they said. "The most awful yet."

To travel downstream by boat was much different from going upstream. Before, the men had to toil against the current, pulling the boats along by ropes, pushing them with poles, their hands blistered and their feet full of thorns.

In one day alone, the first day, we now made ninety-seven miles. We reached Three Forks on the third day.

We did lose some horses to the Crow, who are the best horse thieves anywhere. One misty night they stole up and rode away with half our herd. They could not be followed because the ground was hard and gravelly and left no hoofprints.

The next day the stinging flies were so bad we had to build smoking fires and lather mud on the horses that were left. Our camp was surrounded by buffalo bushes but the red berries were not much good to eat.

The next day was better. We came to a field of prickly pears. The pears were deep purple and ripe. But they grew surrounded by thorns, the big ones that pierced thick leather. Also they were covered with tufts of little thorns, sharp as needles. The men were hungry but looked at the thorns and turned away.

I had eaten many prickly pears. They are full of small hard seeds but the flesh is smooth. It tastes like warm milk when you drink it and dream all the time that you're in a meadow of sweet violets.

There's only one way to fix a prickly pear. You knock it off with a stick, roll it quickly in a fire, and burn off the tufts. I showed the men how to do this and they ate pears until they lay on the ground and groaned.

At Three Forks, Captain Clark divided the party. He took eight men, Charbonneau, me, and the baby with a large herd of horses and struck out to the east to meet Captain Lewis beyond the Rosebud River and the Powder, at the mouth of the Yellowstone.

Before we got there, Captain Clark carved his name on a tall rock we came to beside the river. He held the baby up and pointed to it.

"See, that's my name carved on the rock," he said to Meeko. "And I have named the rock Pompey's Pillar. Do you like it?"

The baby laughed and showed his teeth. Captain Clark had taught him to say American words long before he could speak Shoshone. He thought of Meeko as his son. Tears came to my eyes.

Captain Lewis was not at the mouth of the Yellowstone as he promised to be. We waited a day for him. But the mosquitoes and gnats were so bad that Captain Clark decided to move down the Missouri. He left a note on a tree for Captain Lewis to let him know where we were.

We floated into nests of rattlesnakes. They swarmed everywhere. They even swam in the river, but no one was bitten.

The mosquitoes came with us. They swarmed over our horses and stung them so hard the men had to build big fires and tether the horses in the smoke to keep them from bolting. Sergeant Ordway's eyes swelled shut, as did the baby's. Hunters killed a deer, but it was so thin we could not eat it. The men said that the animal was so poor because the mosquitoes had sucked away all of its blood.

Our problem was now to find Captain Lewis. We floated down the river for half a day, traveling fast, three times as fast as when we pulled and pushed our way up against the current. At noon we heard a shot. It was much louder than the shots of the Shoshone or the Nez Percé or the Flatheads, for these people used only a pinch of powder.

Captain Lewis's men whooped and waved their shirts and fired the air gun, but the news they brought was bad. They had traveled far to the north and run into a band of Blackfeet, who stole some of their horses and nearly killed them in an ambush. Worse, Captain Lewis had learned that the Maria's, the River That Scolds at All the Others, did not flow into the Saskatchewan, the river that flows down from the far north and the rich fur country.

Worse yet, at least to us, Captain Lewis had been shot. As his canoe floated up and we waded out to see him, we found him lying under a blanket beside Scannon. He had been in an accident with Peter Cruzatte. The two men had gone out hunting for meat. Cruzatte, who had weak eyes, mistook Captain Lewis for a deer or something and had shot him in the back.

Captain Lewis was always getting hurt in one way or another, but he was made of iron. By nightfall he was on his feet again and we all started down the river.

We were near Fort Mandan now. The men cleaned their clothes as best they could. But the fringes on their jackets had all been cut off to make strings for their moccasins. They oiled their guns. Captain Lewis set up the cannon and the air gun, ready to fire as soon as the fort came into view.

Chapter Twenty-seven

Captain Lewis fired a cannon at the first sight of the Minnetarees, and all the people ran down to the river. Black Moccasin came to welcome us, but he looked sad as he embraced me. Red Hawk had been killed not long before by the Blackfeet. To mourn his son, he had cut off one of his fingers, as was the custom of the Minnetarees and the Shoshone.

Charbonneau's wife, Otter Woman, came down to the shore. She was carrying a baby in a cradleboard. Charbonneau looked at the baby and seemed pleased until he saw that it was a girl. Then he hunched his shoulders and turned away.

Captain Lewis fired his cannon three times more. He and Captain Clark smoked a peace pipe with the chieftains and invited them to go with them and meet the Great White Father. The chieftains said that they would like to go but were afraid of the Sioux. The Sioux were camped on the river now, not far below, waiting to kill them.

We camped across the river from the village and had many visitors the rest of the day. Le Borgne himself came to visit us. He left his canoe and stood on the shore, casting his eye about. He looked as tall as a tree.

It had been raining a little but now it was steaming hot. Le Borgne wore a heavy buffalo robe, a towering headdress of foxtails and feathers, and around his neck a double circlet of bearclaws.

Ben York said, "The chief's dressed for winter. Maybe this means we'll get a wintry welcome."

Charbonneau said, "One Eye showoff. Mean nothing. All time big, ugly, showoff, dress-up chief."

"My advice to you is to keep your thoughts to yourself," Captain Clark said. "We deal with a dangerous man. At the end of our journey I don't wish to be scalped."

"Not the end," York said. "We still have some long miles to go. We're not in St. Louis yet."

For me it might be the end. My heart sank at the thought. Yet I clung to the hope that Captain Clark would take me with him. He knew that I loved him. He knew that I hated Charbonneau.

After supper that night he gave Charbonneau the money that President Jefferson owed him. It was a piece of paper worth five hundred dollars, Captain Clark said.

Charbonneau put the paper in his jacket and went off to play the Hand Game with Le Borgne. Otter Woman left her baby with me and trailed after him.

They had not been gone long before Captain Clark came to the tent. He took Meeko out of the cradleboard and sat down and held him in his lap. We were outside by the fire.

For a while he played with the baby. He spoke only to him and not to me. But I felt that he was thinking about me. I was sure that he had something he wanted to say before Charbonneau came back.

I waited. The night was full of sounds. Wild birds were calling to each other. The trees and the sky were filled with their cries. Sounds came from the river that Captain Clark and I had traveled together. I waited.

After some time he put Meeko back in the cradleboard and came and sat beside me on the ground. The fire was dying but live embers cast light on his face.

"Pomp has grown fast," he said. "How old is he? Eighteen months, at least."

"Nineteen."

"He'll soon be ready to learn. I would like to take him back to St. Louis and put him in school. I talked to Charbonneau this evening and he thought that it would be a good thing for the boy."

I was disturbed. "The boy is still a baby," I said.

"But he's not too young to start learning American words. I've taught him three words already—'yes,' 'no,' and 'papa.' He takes after you. He learns fast. Remember how you learned to count from one to twenty in only one day?"

"I remember."

I remembered many things. All the days and weeks and months. All the things we had done together.

"You could go to school, too," Captain Clark said. "To a young ladies' school. There's a fine one for young ladies in St. Louis. Some good ones in Washington, where President Jefferson lives."

"What would I learn in a school?"

"To do needlework."

"I can do needlework now. I have sewn you three jackets and five shirts and . . ."

"I mean fine needlework. Like pillows and spreads. Sheets and nice underclothes for yourself."

"I would learn something else?"

"Oh, yes. You'd learn to write, to use all the words that now you can only speak."

"Other things, too?"

"Many. You can jump from a canoe to the shore in one leap. You can climb a cliff. You can run down a deer, though I have never seen you do it. But you haven't learned to dance. Not yet."

"Is dancing important where you are going?"

"Important. American girls love to dance. They dress up in their fancy clothes and dance and dance and dance. All night, sometimes."

"Sometimes until the sun comes up?"

"Often."

"If I learned to sew nice things and write words and dress up and dance all night when I go to this ladies' school, then I would be a lady myself?"

The embers had turned to ashes. But a fire was burning in front of the lodge where Charbonneau and Le Borgne were playing the Hand Game. The fire lit up the sky and cast flickering lights on Captain Clark's face. He was puzzled.

"Then I would be what you call a lady?" I said.

He did not answer.

"Would you like that?" I asked him.

He stared into the ashes. He was uncomfortable.

"You wish me to go to school and become a lady?"

"Not at all. I like you the way you are, Janey."

It was the sound of the words, not what the words said, that made me suddenly remember what Ben York had told me.

"If," he had said, "if a white man marries you, he will be called a squaw-man and people will look down on him."

I had never forgotten his words. I remembered them now.

A gray mist was drifting up from the river. Captain Clark made another fire, using a fuse like the one he had used on the Columbia River with the Neerchokioos. It sputtered and burst into flame. A bitter smell of powder rose around us.

"About the boy," he said. "Of course you would come along, too. He'll need you. What fun you'll have together. And how much he'll learn. You'll be proud of him."

"I am proud of him now."

Captain Clark hesitated. "And how much you'll learn also."

"I am much too old to go to school."

160

"You're still a child."

A child? Is that the way he thought of me? All this last year, all these days and weeks and months we had been together, he had thought of me as a child.

"A beautiful Indian child," he said.

"I am an Indian woman, Captain Clark. An Indian woman who has a child nineteen months old."

He shrugged at my sharp tone and put a stick of wood on the fire. I was quiet. He talked about St. Louis and Washington, where Thomas Jefferson lived. And how after I was through with school I would meet the Great White Chieftain who ruled America. I listened with one ear.

In the midst of all the talking, screams burst out in the lodge. Charbonneau and Otter Woman came back to the tent.

She was blaming him for losing all of his money to Le Borgne, the five hundred dollars Captain Clark had given him. And he blamed her for trying to tell him how he should have handled the plum pits.

They kept on fighting after Captain Clark left, so I took Meeko and went down to the river and crawled into one of the canoes.

I did not sleep. I thought about Captain Clark. I thought about how he wanted me to go to a school and learn things and become a lady. I thought about what Ben York had told me. I remembered his warning. I saw it written across the sky. Also, I thought about Meeko.

Captain Clark would take him to a big place somewhere. He would send him to school and teach him things. Meeko would learn to talk like a white boy. He would grow up and have a lot of hair on his face. He would look like a white man and try to act like a white man. But he never would be a white man. He was a Shoshone!

I would teach Meeko myself. He would learn to run beside a stream all day from dawn until the sunset and never stop once to take a drink. He would learn to put his hand in

161

boiling water and say that it was cold. He would be a Shoshone always!

In the morning Captain Lewis talked to Le Borgne. He told him that if he kept the peace he would be rewarded by the Great White Chief in Washington. And as a proof of his friendship, Captain Lewis gave him his valuable air gun, which pleased Le Borgne so much that he said he would think about keeping the peace.

Captain Lewis gave me a wonderful present, too. It happened that night while I was at the river getting water to cook with.

"Sacagawea," he said. (He never called me Janey.) "You've taken good care of Scannon. You found food for him when food was scarce. You even saved his life. He thinks much more of you than he does of me. If you want him, young lady, he is yours."

"I want him, I want him, Captain Lewis. Can I have him now?"

"Now."

Scannon, thinking of food, followed me to the lodge. Charbonneau was sitting against a tree while Otter Woman stood over him and combed his beard.

"What's dog for?" he asked.

"Captain Lewis gave him to me."

"Shoshone woman, maybe I give you something too. With large stick on head, huh? That dog eats all the time."

Otter Woman turned and eyed Scannon. "He is a plump one. Maybe it's better to keep him for the pot."

"Maybe good idea, Otter Woman."

I slept in the canoe that night with Scannon. Before dawn I put Meeko on my back and went to the long house. I took a sack of pemmican, five cakes of blackberry bread, and some elk fat.

When the herdsman drove the horses down to the river, I followed him. I had to wait a while until he had eaten and was asleep. Then I took a horse and rode out of the village with Scannon at my heels.

As I rode I saw that the canoes were loaded and ready to leave. I caught a glimpse of Captain Clark. He stood on the shore. His red hair shone in the sun. I had not trusted myself to say farewell to him. Now it was too late.

I crossed my wrists and put them over my heart and pressed them together, one on the other. It was a sign of love.

The shortest trail to my people led toward the setting sun. It was shorter, three times shorter, than the way up the Missouri River and the Yellowstone. It was the quick trail the raiders had taken the time they captured Running Deer and me. The same trail Running Deer had taken when she left and went home.

There was a half moon. I rode hard along the river until the moon set and my guiding star shone through the trees. Scannon ran beside me.

In the morning we were on the trail at sunrise. The sky was deep blue and cloudless. Locusts sang in the high grass. The wild blooms of summer were everywhere. I picked a handful for Meeko.

He laughed and smelled them. One day when he was older I would tell him that the wild blooms were the footprints of little children, those who had gone away and had come back to gladden us. I would tell him many things that the Shoshone people knew.

ABOUT THE AUTHOR

Scott O'Dell was a Newbery Medalist, a three-time Newbery Honor Book winner, a two-time winner of the German "Jugenbuchpreis", winner of the deGrummond and Regina medals, and a recipient of the Hans Christian Andersen Author Medal, the highest international recognition for a body of work by an author of children's books.

Other Scott O'Dell books for Fawcett Juniper are ALEXANDRA, THE CASTLE IN THE SEA, THE ROAD TO DAMIETTA, THE SPANISH SMILE, and THE SERPENT NEVER SLEEPS.

Mr. O'Dell died in 1989.